THE JOURNEY OF XIAO TAO

THE JOURNEY OF XIAO TAO

With 366 Chinese Idioms to Kick
the Chinese-learning Difficulty Away

Yisheng Lan

Xlibris Corporation

To order additional copies of this book, contact:
Xlibris Corporation
1-888-795-4274
www.Xlibris.com
Orders@Xlibris.com
132592

CONTENTS

WHY I WROTE THIS BOOK

Many people outside of China are eager to learn Chinese. Chinese language has become a popular subject to study.

However, the Chinese language is quite different from other major languages. More than a few people had started learning but later gave up because of the difficulties with the language.

There should be an easy solution to the Chinese-learning difficulties.

I still remember when I was only five or six years old, I was often captivated by my father's stories about Chinese idioms. Since then I have made progress in learning Chinese by leaps and bounds. Based on my personal experience, I believe the quickest and most effective way to learn Chinese is through the learning of Chinese idioms.

Let's analogize learning Chinese to driving a car.

A car running at a speed of 30 MPH needs an hour to cover a distance of 30 miles. It needs only half an hour to pass a shortcut of 15 miles to reach the same destination. However, if it goes on an expressway, it may only need a quarter of an hour.

To learn Chinese, the shortcut lies in learning idioms. In the Chinese language, there are numerous very vivid idioms. Chinese idioms are not just juggles of words; they are very much the heart and soul of the language.

This book is especially designed for people with a bit of Chinese-learning background. It will aid in readers' learning interest, enhance their learning confidence and increase their learning speed. In brief, this book will help readers persist in learning Chinese until they are successful.

Moreover, it is much easier to learn Chinese through the reading of an interesting story than laboring through a textbook.

This book is about a naughty boy who goes on an adventurous journey where he meets many fantastic characters, experiences many unusual affairs and learns a lot.

The story uses and connects a series of 366 most frequently used Chinese idioms. Through reading and remembering this interesting story, readers can learn Chinese with joy and ease, just like driving on a short expressway while listening to one's favorite music.

Actually, this book may function as a combination of a storybook and a textbook with story in the main body and text in the notes. Readers can enjoy the story while learning idioms at the same time and on the same page.

There are 365 or 366 days in a year, and there are 366 most frequently used Chinese idioms in this book. By learning, remembering and trying to use one idiom a day and reviewing and practicing day-to-day, in just one year, readers will be able to understand basic Chinese.

An idiom a day kicks the Chinese-learning difficulty away.

For readers' convenience, at the end of this book I summarized all idioms mentioned in the story.

Please enjoy this book. It is a reward for your appreciation of the great and brilliant Chinese culture.

Yisheng Lan (蓝绎圣)

THE KEY OF THIS BOOK—
HOW TO USE THE NOTES

A. Forms of Chinese Characters

There are two forms of Chinese character; the standardized form (i.e. the traditional form or the original complex form) and the simplified form. The former has been used for thousands of years, and currently mainly in Taiwan, Hong Kong, Macau and overseas. The latter has been adopted in Mainland China since January 28, 1956. However, its popularity is growing worldwide.

This book mainly uses the simplified form, but it also includes the standardized form by putting it in the brackets "[ ]." For many characters, their simplified form and their standardized form are the same, and therefore no bracket is needed.

B. For Individual Characters

Following each individual Chinese character is a Chinese Pinyin notation (mandarin Pronunciation) with four tones marked in Chinese ways, and then is the English pronunciation.

The four tones of modern standard Chinese pronunciation are ❶ 阴 [陰] 平 yīn píng (high and level tone; the first of the four tones in modern standard Chinese pronunciation), ❷ 阳 [陽] 平 yáng píng (rising tone, the second of the four tones in modern standard Chinese pronunciation), ❸ 上声 [聲] shǎng shēng (falling-rising tone, the third tone in modern standard Chinese pronunciation) and ❹ 去声 [聲] qù shēng (falling tone; the fourth tone in modern standard Chinese pronunciation).

11

For instance, in Chinese phonetic system "e" has four tones as ❶ ē; ❷ é; ❸ ě and ❹ è.†

After the Chinese Pinyin notation are two dividing lines "‖", and after the dividing lines is the English pronunciation. For simplicity, this book does not list the four tones of the English pronunciation. Through looking at the Chinese Pinyin notation (at the left side of the dividing lines "‖") reader are able to know the tone for the character in English pronunciation.

After the English pronunciation is a back slash "\" and after the back slash is the English explanation of the Chinese character.

Take the first character 杀 of Idiom #16 杀鸡取卵 as an example.

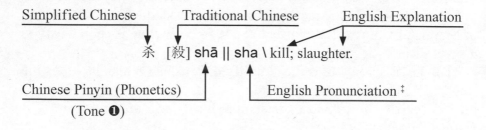

Then take the third character 取 of the same idiom as another example.

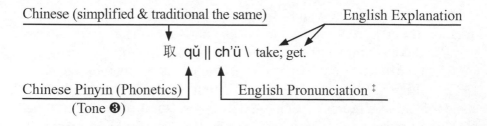

---

†   For correct Chinese pronunciations, I suggest reader to buy a Chinese word processor program such as NJStar (from http://www.njstar.com) which has audio functions and provides accurate mandarin pronunciations when entering Chinese Pinying notations in the computers.

‡   There are several English Pronunciation Systems. This book uses Wade System, which is popular.

C. For Each Idiom

Following a colon is the word-for-word or literal translation. Sometimes after a semicolon is the free translation. Sometimes there are more than one semicolon, and the more semicolons, the closer to Standard English. Sometimes there is a dash, and after the dash is the direct explanation of the idiom or an equivalent English idiom.

Let's still take the above-mentioned Idiom #16 杀鸡取卵 as an example.

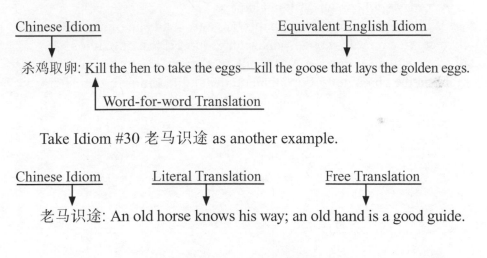

Chinese Idiom

Equivalent English Idiom

杀鸡取卵: Kill the hen to take the eggs—kill the goose that lays the golden eggs.

Word-for-word Translation

Take Idiom #30 老马识途 as another example.

Chinese Idiom   Literal Translation   Free Translation

老马识途: An old horse knows his way; an old hand is a good guide.

****

It is important for reader of this book to keep in mind that, like English, most Chinese characters have more than one distinct meaning. Often times, the meaning of a single Chinese character changes when it is combined with another Chinese character. In this book, most of the idioms are formed through combination of many Chinese characters. As a result, the meanings harbored by the Chinese characters within the idioms may differ greatly from the meanings of these same characters if they were standing on their own.

For simplicity reasons and to avoid readers' confusion, for each Chinese character, this book by and large only lists the most relevant meanings to the underlying idioms. It does not list other uses or meaning of that particular character, even if those uses or meanings are more common. As a result, it is recommended that the readers focus more on learning and understanding the entire idioms rather than memorizing the meanings of single Chinese characters.

In addition, single Chinese characters may also be combined to form a "character group" (i.e. a phrase) which typically consist of two Chinese character (in contrast, idiom usually consist of four or more Chinese characters). The meaning of a single Chinese character may also change once it is used in a character group. For example, the Chinese character "工" means "work" and the Chinese character "夫" means "man." However, when combined together, the character group "工夫" means "effort." (Please see Idioms # 84 for reference.) Just as idioms are the heart and soul of the Chinese language, character group are also frequently used in everyday spoken and written Chinese.

While most of the idioms in this book are made up of single Chinese characters,, some also contain character groups. (Please see Idiom #28 "投机" for another reference.) As a result, readers are also encourage to focus more on the character groups than on the single Chinese characters.

§1

Xiao Tao, A New Arrival of the Fairy World

Everyone called him 小淘 (Xiao Tao, xiǎo táo ‖ siao tao). Actually, "Xiao Tao" was neither a formal name nor a pet name. It was merely a nickname, and it meant "little naughty (boy)."

This red-haired boy was a little taller and bigger than the other boys with the same age, and comparatively 眉清目秀.[1] Xiao Tao's only strange thing was, five red hairs stood on the top of his head, with one in the center like a pivot and four around it spaced evenly as if indicating the four directions in a compass.

According to the midwife's recollection, when delivering the infant, she saw a red hair, and the entire room suddenly became bright reddish. She used obstetric forceps to grip the hair, and a whitish and chubby baby followed out!

The baby cried loudly, and apparently was a healthy one. "I delivered hundreds of babies, but none had red hair. This boy is out of the ordinary, and will 出人头地[2] in the future!" Said the midwife in front of everybody.

Xiao Tao had two elder sisters 大妞 (Da Niu, dà niū ‖ ta niu, which meant "the first girl") and 二妞 (Er Niu, èr niū ‖ êrh niu, which meant "the second girl"), and they were all thin and small. Xiao Tao

---

[1] 眉 méi ‖ mei \ eyebrow; brow. 清 qīng ‖ ch'ing \ unmixed; clear; distinct. 目 mù ‖ mu \ eye. 秀 xiù ‖ hsiu \ elegant; beautiful. 眉清目秀: Have delicate features; be remarkably handsome; good-looking. (Idiom #1)

[2] 出 chū ‖ ch'u \ go or come out; exceed. 人 rén ‖ jên \ person; people. 头 [頭] tóu ‖ t'ou \ head; top. 地 dì ‖ ti \ field; ground; place; position. 出人 头地; Rise above others—be a VIP. (Idiom #2)

grew every day and every night, and before long his weight was the sum of his sisters.

Neighbors all said that this boy had good luck, and he would be a high-ranking official, make big fortune, and 光宗耀祖.[3] They suggested his parents to let him study a lot.

---

[3] 光 guāng || kuang \ honor. 宗 zōng || tsung \ ancestor; clan. 耀 yào || yao \ honor. 祖 zǔ || tsu \ grandparent; ancestor. 光宗耀祖: Bring honor to one's forefathers. (Idiom #3)

§2

Xiao Tao Waited Hares to Come Again and Again

Xiao Tao's parents were farmers at the foot of Guan Tian Mountain, in a typical 鱼米之乡.[4]His father did farming all his life, was very tired, and hoped Xiao Tao to grow fast and become his good helper. However, his mother hoped him to study well, because being a "blind man with eyes wide open"—an illiterate person was painful.

Xiao Tao studied at an elementary school. He did not study hard, and was too fond of playing. After returning home he did not do homework and therefore his school reports were 一塌糊涂,[5]but he did not care about them.

Everyday after school he went back home to read children's picture-story books, and after supper he slept with thunderous snores. He often dreamed, and a variety of strange people and matters mushroomed in his dreams. He sometimes laughed, sometimes cried, and sometimes shouted aloud. Mom asked what he had dreamed, but he often said, "Heaven's secrets must not be given away."

When Xiao Tao was eleven, his dad taught him to sow seeds in the field, but he did not want to learn. Dad then went to the town.

---

[4] 鱼[魚] yú || yü \ fish. 米 mǐ || mi \ rice. 之 zhī || chih \ <auxiliary word> (used to connect the modifier and the word it modifies) 乡[鄉] xiāng || hsiang \ countryside; native place. 鱼米之乡: A land of fish and rice; a fertile land—a land of plenty. (Idiom #4)

[5] 一 yī || i \ whole; all. 塌 tā || t'a \ collapse. 糊 hū || hu \ paste; trouble. 涂 [塗] tú || t'u \ spread; smear. 糊涂: Messy; confusing; muddled. 一塌糊涂: Very bad; awful; terrible—in a complete mess. (Idiom #5)

One day Xiao Tao saw a wild dog chasing a hare. The hare hit the trunk of a big tree, and died instantly. The dog smelled at the dead hare and left. Xiao Tao picked up the hare, brought it home and let mom make it into food.

Mom's heart was filled with joy. They had eaten veggies everyday, but today they could eat meat. Mom told a story to little Xiao Tao about hares as she prepared the hare's meat.

"Across the river in the mountain there was a hunter. He had a hunting dog. The hunting dog helped the hunter to catch hares, and they could catch a big bag of hares. The hunting dog worked very well, and the hunter gave him a lot of hare meat to eat.

The amount of hares became fewer and fewer, and the dog turned idler and idler.

兔子尾巴长不了.[6]This situation could not last long. Eventually, one day they could not find even one hare. The hunter and his dog sought hares for three days, but they found nothing. The 饥肠辘辘[7]hunter killed the no more useful hunting dog, cooked him and ate him. This is called '兔死狗烹'."[8]

Xiao Tao ate a lot of hare meat. He said to mom, "I do not need to learn farming. I can catch hares. I do not need a hunting dog. Hares will automatically deliver themselves to my doorstep." Mom said he was 痴

---

[6] 兔 tù || t'u \ hare; rabbit. 子 zi || tsŭ \ (noun suffix). 兔子: hare; rabbit. 尾 wěi || wei \ tail; end. 巴 ba || pa \ cling to; stick to. 尾巴: tail. 长[長] cháng || ch'ang \ long. 不 bù || pu \ no; not. 了 liǎo || liao \ <auxiliary word>. 兔子尾巴长不了; The tail of a hare (or a rabbit) can't be long—it will not be long-lasting. (Idiom #6)

[7] 饥[飢 or 饑] jī || chi \ be hungry; starve; famish; famine. 肠[腸] cháng || ch'ang \ intestines. 辘 [轆] lù || lu \ the rumbling sound. 饥肠辘辘: One's stomach growling with hunger. (Idiom #7)

[8] 兔 tù || t'u \ hare; rabbit. 死 sǐ || ssŭ \ die; to the death. 狗 gǒu || kou \ dog. 烹 pēng || p'êng \ boil; cook. 兔死狗烹: Kill the hunting dogs for food once the hares are bagged; get rid of one's allies once they are no longer useful. (Idiom #8)

人说梦,[9]but Xiao Tao said, "My fortune is especially good. I am different from the others. I have five red hairs, while the others have none."

Since then Xiao Tao 守株待兔[10]everyday. Unfortunately, after waiting for half a month, he did not even see any trace of a hare at all.

---

[9] 痴 chī || ch'ih \ mad; silly; idiotic. 人 rén || jên \ person; people. 说[說] shuō|| shuo \ speak; talk; say; chat; gossip. 梦[夢]mèng || mêng \ dream. 痴人说梦: A madman talks about his dreams; talking nonsense; dreaming about unrealistic things. (Idiom #9)

[10] 守 shǒu || shou \ keep watch; close to; near. 株 zhū || chu \ trunk of a tree; stem of a plant. 待 dài || tai \ wait for; await. 兔 tù || t'u \ hare; rabbit. 守株待兔: Stand by a stump waiting for more hares to come and dash themselves against the stump; depend on luck or fortune. (Idiom #10)

§3

Xiao Tao Left Home without Saying Good-bye

Xiao Tao suddenly remembered: when dad was leaving, he was told to sow seeds in the field, but he had forgotten. He then 手忙脚乱[11]sowed seeds. Seedlings grew very slowly because he had sowed them in a delayed time.

For fear of dad's rebuke, he quietly got up at wee hours to 拔苗助长.[12]

Two days later, dad came back home and saw seedlings all lying down in the field with their roots exposed in the air. He knew that Xiao Tao had done this.

Dad asked Xiao Tao why he had made this mess, and wanted him to admit his fault. Xiao Tao did not acknowledge his mistake, and said that this had been the hares' fault: because hares had not hit against the trunk again, he had to wait for them; otherwise he would not have pulled the seedlings upward, and would not have been criticized by dad.

Dad was so angry that he boxed Xiao Tao's ears.

---

[11] 手 shǒu || shou \ hand. 忙 máng || mang \ busy; hurry. 脚 jiǎo || chiao \ foot. 乱[亂] luàn || luan \ in disorder; in a mess; in confusion. 手忙脚乱: With one's hand and feet disorderly busy; hastily; hurriedly. (Idiom #11)

[12] 拔 bá || pa \ pull out; pull up. 苗 miáo || miao \ seedling; young plant. 助 zhù || chu \ help; assist; aid. 长[長] zhǎng || chang \ grow; develop. 拔苗助长: Try to help the seedlings grow by pulling them upward—extreme eagerness which leads to a bad result. (Idiom #12)

Xiao Tao did not cry. As a brave and unbending boy, he decided to go from home and to 游山玩水,[13]闯荡江湖.[14]

Xiao Tao quietly prepared his luggage—a parcel with clothes, a cap, a pair of shoes, a pair of straw sandals, two bowls, a pair of chopsticks, and a towel, etc. He knew many travelers brought umbrellas with them, but he did not need one, because he had a big head, which could shield his body fairly well when raining.

"Do I need a compass?" Xiao Tao asked himself. "We do not have one at home, and I do not have the money to buy one," Xiao Tao thought, "just forget about it, since my head is a nice compass itself!"

He took a piece of paper and a red crayon, and wrote a note: "I go out to learn more. Don't worry about me. Take care of yourselves." He then drew a circle to symbolize his head, and added five hairs on the head. This was his "signature." In addition, he took some money from a drawer.

He put his note on the kitchen table, and left home. But he soon returned to take his bamboo tube. Inside the tube there was a cricket—his favorite insect. The cricket became his traveling companion for the entire journey.

[13] 游[遊] yóu || yu \ tour; travel. 山 shān || shan \ mountain; hill. 玩 wán || wan \ play; have fun; enjoy. 水 shuǐ || shui \ water; a general term for rivers, lakes, seas, etc. 游山玩水: Travel and sightsee; visit various scenic spots. (Idiom #13)

[14] 闯[闖] chuǎng || ch'uang \ rush; dash; charge. 荡[蕩] dàng || tang \ loaf about. 江 jiāng || chiang \ river. 湖 hú || hu \ lake. 闯荡江湖: Make a living wandering from place to place; be a vagabond. (Idiom #14)

§4

Old Fisherman Benefited from Snipe and Clam's Fighting

Xiao Tao walked ten *li* (1 *li* = 0.5 kilometer = ~ 0.31 mile) eastward. He felt hungry. Seeing an old fisherman sitting by a pond, he asked for food. The tall and strong fisherman said, "You help me to catch fish, and then I will invite you to my home to eat smoked fish."

Xiao Tao felt that to fish with a hook and line was too time-consuming. He climbed onto a tree near the pond to catch fish. The old fisherman laughed loudly. He said, "If you climb a tree to catch cicadas, or to collect birds' eggs, it might be hopeful. Nothing can be more foolish than to 缘木求鱼!"[15]

Xiao Tao also felt himself a little too unwise. To show his cleverness, he started to scoop up water from the pond by means of a bamboo basket. Xiao Tao said, "You can only get several fish, but I will get all fish of the entire pond!"

The old fisherman said, "杀鸡取卵,[16]you can get many eggs, but later you will get zero egg. Drain the pond, you can get all the fish, but later you will get zero fish. A man should 目光远大,[17]and should not be shortsighted."

---

[15] 缘[緣] yuán || yüan \ along. 木 mù || mu \ tree; timber; wood. 求 qiú || ch'iu \ seek; strive for; request; demand. 鱼[魚]yú || yü \ fish. 缘木求鱼: Climb a tree to catch fish—a useless and foolish method. (Idiom #15)

[16] 杀[殺] shā || sha \ kill; slaughter. 鸡[雞] jī || chi \ chicken. 取 qǔ || ch'ü \ take; get. 卵 luǎn || luan \ egg. 杀鸡取卵: Kill the hen to take the eggs—kill the goose that lays the golden eggs. (Idiom #16)

[17] 目 mù || mu \ eye. 光 guāng || kuang \ light; ray. 目光: Sight; vision; view. 远[遠] yuǎn || yüan \ far; distant; remote. 大 dà || ta \ big; large; great.

Xiao Tao did not listen to the old fisherman's persuasion, and went on scooping water until he was dripping with sweat. However, the water level in the pond kept unchanged. Said the fisherman, "竹篮打水一场空.[18]You should not 徒劳无功."[19]

By that time the old fisherman had already caught a lot of fish, and was preparing to go back his home with Xiao Tao before they saw a snipe was fighting fiercely with a big clam.

The snipe used his long beak to peck the soft tissue of the clam, while the clam used his shells to clamp the beak of the snipe. The old fisherman said while laughing, "鹬蚌相争, 渔翁得利."[20]He picked up the snipe by his right hand and the clam by his left hand, put them into his bamboo basket, and then covered and fastened the basket with a string bag.

远大: Long-range; broad; ambitious. 目光远大: Be farsighted; think about the future; have a broader vision. (Idiom #17)

[18] 竹 zhú || chu \ bamboo. 篮 [籃] lán || lan \ basket. 打 dǎ || ta \ draw. 水 shuǐ || shui \ water. 一 yī || i \ one. 场 [場]cháng || ch'ang \ <measure word> spell; period. 空 kōng || k'ung \ in vain; empty; hollow. 一场空: All in vain; futile. 竹篮打水一场空: Draw water with a bamboo basket—ineffective; unproductive. (Idiom #18)

[19] 徒劳无功 tú || t'u \ empty; bare; merely; only. 劳[勞] láo || lao \ work; labor. 无[無] wú || wu \ nothing; nil; not have; there is not; without. 功 gōng || kung \ result; achievement. 徒劳无功: spend energy to achieve nothing. (Idiom #19)

[20] 鹬 [鷸] yù || yü \ snipe; sandpiper. 蚌 bàng || pang \ clam; freshwater mussel. 相 xiāng || hsiang \ mutually; each other; one another. 争 zhēng || chêng \ contend; vie. 渔 yú || yü \ fishing; fishery. 翁 wēng || wêng \ old man. 得 dé || tê \ get, obtain, gain. 利 lì || li \ profit; interest. 鹬蚌相争, 渔翁得利: When the snipe and the clam grapple, it is the fisherman who stands to benefit—a third party benefits from a fight. (Idiom #20)

IDIOM #20

IDIOM #24

24

§5

Xiao Tao Saw Beans Climbing
and Crying in a Pot

Xiao Tao followed the old fisherman home. The old man let his wife prepare the dinner. Xiao Tao 自告奋勇[21]to light a fire to cook rice.

The fisherman's wife was a hospitable woman. She said, "We will have smoked fish, roasted snipe and clam soup, but we lack a vegetable. Let me make a bowl of soybeans."

She poured water and soybeans into a pot, and put beanstalks into the chamber of the cooking stove. Two soybeans dropped on the top of the kitchen range. The beanstalks were quickly burnt. Xiao Tao helped to add new beanstalks into the chamber, and used a worn-out palm fan to fan the flames.

Suddenly sad and shrill cries burst out from inside the pot, and gave everyone a scare. Xiao Tao opened the lid, and only saw soybeans were 争先恐后[22]climbing up the pot to escape outwards.

The old fisherman's wife hurried to shut down the lid. The beans continued their climbing and crying. Xiao Tao could not bear the beans'

---

[21] 自 zì || tsŭ\ self; one's own. 告 gào || kao \ declare; inform. 奋[奮] fèn || fên \ exert oneself; act vigorously. 勇 yǒng || yung \ brave; courageous. 自告奋勇: Voluntarily assume a tough task. (Idiom #21)

[22] 争[爭] zhēng || chêng \ contend; vie; strive. 先 xiān || hsien \ earlier; first; in advance. 恐 kǒng || k'ung \ be afraid of; fear; intimidate. 后[後] hòu || hou \ behind; back; rear; after. 争先恐后: Strive to be the first and fear to lag behind; struggle to be the first. (Idiom #22)

tragic death, and 釜底抽薪.[23]However, since the pot was already too hot, the beans still passed away. A bowl of half cooked soybeans was put on the dining table.

The old fisherman said to Xiao Tao, "This is called 煮豆燃其.[24]Do you know the original source of it?" Xiao Tao shook his head.

"Many years ago there was an emperor called 曹丕 (Cao Pi, cáo pī || ts'ao p'i, 187-226). His younger brother 曹植 (Cao Zhi, cáo zhí || ts'ao chih, 192-232) could write very good poems. One day Cao Pi ordered Cao Zhi to compose a poem—on pain of death in case of failure—an impromptu poem within the set time of walking seven paces."

"The younger brother composed an extempore verse as he sobbed, and completed a good poem within seven paces.

> 煮豆燃豆其, (Cooking beans while burning beanstalks,)
> 豆在釜中泣. (Beans cried in the pan with desperate tears.)
> '本是同根生, ('We were growing up out of the same roots,)
> 相煎何太急?' (Why do you fry me so hurried and ruthless?')"

Xiao Tao asked, "Then the younger brother was not beheaded. Right?"

"Yes."

"He had good luck. If I were the emperor, I would also have ordered my younger brother to make a poem within seven paces. If he had succeeded, I would have ordered him to make another poem within six paces, until he was beheaded."

---

[23] 釜 fǔ || fu \ ancient wok. 底 dǐ || ti \ bottom; base. 抽 chōu || ch'ou \ take out (from in between); take (a part from a whole). 薪 xīn || hsin \ firewood; fuel. 釜底抽薪: Take away the firewood from under the wok—get to the root of the problem; get rid of a problem completely. (Idiom #23)

[24] 煮 zhǔ || chu \ boil; cook. 豆 dòu || tou \ beans; peas. 燃 rán || jan \ burn; ignite; light. 其 qí || ch'i \ beanstalk. 煮豆燃其: Burn beanstalks to cook beans—persecution within the same family. (Idiom #24)

The old fisherman and his wife 不约而同[25]said: "Why are you so heartless?"

Xiao Tao talked back, "Only heartless persons could achieve a lot. Most softhearted people are good-for-nothing!" He even added to the old fisherman, "You are kindhearted, and therefore you can only be a fisherman; I am hardhearted, and I may be an emperor in the future!"

The old fisherman and his wife 付之一笑[26]aloud, and they both said that the boy 不知天高地厚.[27]

Xiao Tao felt that he and the old couple 话不投机半句多.[28]After dinner he just rubbed his lips and left. He neither expressed his thankfulness nor said goodbye to his hosts.

---

[25] 不 bù || pu \ no; not. 约[約] yuē || yüeh \ make an appointment; arrange; ask or invite in advance. 而 ér || êrh \ and yet; but. 同 tóng || t'ung \ same; alike; similar; be the same as; together; in common. 不约而同: Having the same thought or taking the same action simultaneously. (Idiom #25)

[26] 付 fù || fu \ commit to; pay. 之 zhī || chih \ <pronoun> (used in place of an object). 一 yī || i \ one; single. 笑 xiào || hsiao \ laugh; smile. 付之一笑: Pass it off with a laugh. (Idiom #26)

[27] 不 bù || pu \ no; not. 知 zhī || chīh \ know; realize; be aware of. 天 tian || t'ien\ sky; day. 高 gāo || kao \ tall; high. 地 dì || ti \ the earth; land. 厚 hòu || hou \ thick; deep. 不知天高地厚: Do not know the height of the heavens and the depth of the earth; do not know the ways of the world—overly confident in oneself. (Idiom #27)

[28] 话[話] huà || hua \ speech; talk. 不 bù || pu \ no; not. 投 tóu || t'ou \ agree with; fit in with. 机[機] jī || chi \ chance; occasion; opportunity. 投机: congenial; agreeable. 半 bàn || pan \ half; semi-. 句 jù || chü \ sentence. 多 duō || to \ many; much; more. 话不投机半句多: Since there is no common ground, a half sentence is a waste of time; have nothing in common to talk about.(Idiom #28)

§6

Xiao Tao Mounted a White Horse

Xiao Tao entered a grove, and lost his way before long. He had wanted to go to the West Lake at the east side, but he went to the East Lake at the west side. Fortunately there was a young man sitting on a big rock. Xiao Tao went ahead to ask the way. The young man said, "Please do not jeer at my disability. I am sorry for unable to guide your way." He was a blind man.

Xiao Tao embarrassingly said sorry, and went around the woods. He then understood that 问道于盲[29] would get no answer.

Coincidentally an old white horse came out from the woods. Xiao Tao remembered that mom once said, "老马识途."[30] He then ran to the horse and sat on the back of him. The old horse was very friendly and let Xiao Tao be a rider.

The horse walked unhurriedly. Xiao Tao was eager to go to the West Lake, but the horse walked while gnawing grass by the road. He was very hungry.

---

[29] 问[問] wèn || wên \ ask; inquire. 道 dào || tao \ road, way, path. 于 yú || yü \ from. 盲 máng || mang \ blind. 问道于盲: Ask way from a blind person—try to obtain advice from a person who knows nothing. (Idiom #29)

[30] 老 lǎo || lao \ old; aged; experienced, veteran. 马[馬] mǎ || ma \ horse. 识 [識] shí || shih \ know; knowledge. 途 tú || t'u \ way; road; route. 老马识途: An old horse knows his way; an old hand is a good guide. (Idiom #30)

Xiao Tao implored the old horse, "Could you please go faster?" The old horse turned his head, stared at Xiao Tao and said with a little discontentment, "又要马儿跑得快, 又要马儿不吃草.[31]Will it do?"

Xiao Tao knew that it was he who had to look to the horse for help, and he could do nothing but wait. After the horse was full, he dashed along the way and brought Xiao Tao to the shore of the West Lake.

---

[31] 又 yòu || yu \ also; again; in addition. 要 yào || yao \ want; ask for; wish. 马[馬] mǎ || ma \ horse. 儿[兒] r || r \ <linguistic suffixation>. 跑 pǎo ||p'ao \ run; run away. 得 de || tê \ <auxiliary word> (to link a verb or an adjective to a complement which describes the manner or degree). 快 kuài || k'uai \ fast; quick. 不 bù || pu \ no; not. 吃 chī || ch'ih \ eat. 草 cǎo || ts'ao \ grass; straw. 又要马儿跑得快, 又要马儿不吃草: Expect a horse to run fast but not let it graze—eat one's cake and have it too. (Idiom #31)

§7

Xiao Tao Quenched His Thirst
by Thinking of Plums

Someone was selling fried rice at the lakeshore. Xiao Tao wanted to buy one bowl, but he grudged paying for it because his journey would be pretty long and he should save money for the future. Suddenly he remembered that when eating fish at the old fisherman's home, he had put two fish eyes into his pocket. He felt in his pocket for a while and found that the two fish eyes were still there. He tapped his head and formed an evil plan.

He entered a pawnshop and tried to pawn the fish eyes off as pearls.

The pawnbroker said, "Child, do you want to 鱼目混珠?"[32]With a grab he caught Xiao Tao.

Xiao Tao cried and begged for mercy. The pawnbroker felt the child was a clever kid, and released him. In addition, he gave Xiao Tao five 钱 (*qian* [one *qian* = 3.125 grams or 0.1102 ounce]) silver.

Xiao Tao used one *qian* to buy a big bowl of fried rice, 狼吞虎咽[33]it, and then started to go eastward.

---

[32] 鱼[魚] yú || yü \ fish. 目 mù || mu \ eye. 混 hùn || hun \ mix; confuse; pass off as. 珠 zhū || chu \ pearl; jewel; bead. 鱼目混珠: Pass off fish eyes as pearls—pass off a fake object as the real thing; defraud; deceive. (Idiom #32)

[33] 狼 láng || lang \ wolf. 吞 tūn || t'un \ swallow; gulp down. 虎 hǔ || hu \ tiger. 咽 yàn || yen \ swallow. 狼吞虎咽: Wolf down; devour; eat greedily. (Idiom #33)

The more he went the thirstier he felt. The thirstier he felt the more tiresome he appeared.

He saw a roadside pavilion, and inside the pavilion a big fellow was drinking water. He went to ask for water, but the big fellow said, "You came a little too late. I just drank all water in the bottle gourd."

Xiao Tao borrowed a pickaxe and a shovel from the big man, and started to dig a well over there. "I bet there is water underground," Xiao Tao pouted his little lips and said. The big man laughed loudly. "临渴掘井[34]will make you thirst to death before you dig to half the depth!"

The big man asked Xiao Tao, "Have you ever eaten plums?" "Yes. Green plums were very sour, but ripened ones were sweet." "There is a green plum grove ahead. You may eat your fill over there."

Xiao Tao thought of the sour taste of green plums, a lot of saliva secreted out, and wetted his mouth. He felt no more thirsty. This was the trick of 望梅止渴.[35]

---

[34] 临[臨] lín || lin \ on the point of; just before; be about to. 渴 kě || k'ê \ thirsty. 掘 jué || chüeh \ dig. 井 jǐng || ching \ well. 临渴掘井: Not dig a well until one is thirsty—a belated attempt. (Idiom #34)

[35] 望 wàng || wang \ hope; expect. 梅 méi || mei \ plum. 止 zhǐ || chih \ stop. 渴 kě || k'ê \ thirsty. 望梅止渴: Quench one's thirst by thinking of plums—soothe oneself through imagination (usually in a difficult situation). (Idiom #35)

§8

A Fox Let Xiao Tao to Ask
a Tiger for His Skin

The sky was getting dark. When Xiao Tao was worrying about how to spend the night, he met a female fox.

Xiao Tao knew that foxes were despicable creatures, and did not want to strike up a conversation with her. However, the fox had seen Xiao Tao's four *qian* of silver in his small parcel, and tried to obtain it.

The fox said, "Xiao Tao, your skin is too thin. In case you fall down and break the skin on your head, your red hairs will have nothing to adhere to. If all your five hairs come off, you will no more be Xiao Tao, and you will die!"

Xiao Tao thought, 皮之不存, 毛将焉附?[36] He felt what the fox had warned was reasonable. Then what could he do? He got alarmed.

The fox 眉头一皱, 计上心来.[37] She said, "Oh, I have a good idea! You should go immediately to Great King Tiger to ask for help. He will

---

[36] 皮 pí || p'i \ skin; hide; fur. 之 zhī || chih \ <auxiliary word> (used between the subject and the predicate so as to make it nominative) 不 bù || pu \ no; not. 存 cún || ts'un \ exist. 毛 máo || mao \ hair. 将 jiāng || chiang \ be going to; be about to; will; shall. 焉 yān || yen \ how; why, what. 附 fù || fu \ attach; add; depend on. 皮之不存,毛将焉附: With the skin gone, what can the hair adhere to ?—One depends on another to survive. (Idiom #36)

[37] 眉 méi || mei \ eyebrow. 头[頭] tóu || t'ou \ head. 眉头 brows. 一 yī|| i \ one. 皱[皺] zhòu || chou \ wrinkle; crease. 计[計] jì || chi \ idea; stratagem; plan. 上 shàng || shang \ go up; go ahead; up; upward. 心 xīn || hsin \

soon come. A tiger has big body with thick skin. It will be no problem for him to give you a little skin."

Xiao Tao said, "Even if I were as bold as a panther, I still dare not 与虎谋皮!"[38]

The fox said, "Great King Tiger is my good friend, and I am his military adviser. You give me two *qian* of silver, and I will help you to borrow skin from him."

Xiao Tao said, "I do not want to borrow skin from a tiger. I only need to be cautious not to fall and not to break my skin. My hairs will not come off, and I will still be Xiao Tao!"

But the fox said, "It won't do. A tiger likes to eat children the best. Especially your red hairs are just like fine shreds of carrot on a roasted beefsteak, which will greatly enhance his appetite. If you do not give me the money, I will tell Great King Tiger to eat you!"

狐假虎威[39]made Xiao Tao be frightened to 魂不附体.[40]He had to obediently take out two *qian of* silver from his parcel and passed it to the fox.

---

heart; mind. 来[來] **lái** || **lai** \ come; arrive. 眉头一皱,计上心来: Knit the brows and a plan comes to one's mind; to plot a plan. (Idiom #37)

[38] 与[與] **yǔ** || **yü** \ <preposition> (used to introduce the recipient of an action) 虎 **hǔ** || **hu** \ tiger. 谋[謀] **móu** || **mou** \ consult; seek. 皮 **pí** || **p'i** \ skin, hide; fur. 与虎谋皮: Ask a tiger for its skin—ask someone (usually an evil person) to act counter to his own welfare. (Idiom #38)

[39] 狐 **hú** || **hu** \ fox. 假 **jiǎ** || **chia** \ borrow. 虎 **hǔ** || **hu** \ tiger. 威 **wēi** || **wei** \ impressive strength; might; power. 狐假虎威: The fox borrows the tiger's fierceness (by joining in the tiger's company)—obtain power by association with powerful individuals. (Idiom #39) (Drawing for this idiom is on front cover.)

[40] 魂 **hún** || **hun** \ soul; spirit. 不 **bù** || **pu** \ no; not. 附 **fù** || **fu** \ attach; enclose. 体[體] **tǐ** || **t'i** \ body. 魂不附体: Feel as if one's soul had left one's body—be frightened out of one's wits. (Idiom #40)

§9

Xiao Tao Picked up Two Sesame Seeds but Overlooked a Watermelon

After parting from the fox Xiao Tao hastily went eastwards. By that time night already fell. He was thirsty and hungry again, and wanted to use the remaining two *qian* of silver to buy some food. However, all he saw was farmland with no village ahead and no inn behind. He had to 忍饥挨饿.[41]

Now Xiao Tao really felt that at home he had been in comfort, away from home he was in constant trouble. But he did not retreat.

At that time someone tapped Xiao Tao on his shoulder. He turned his head, looked back and found a farmer in his 30s or 40s looking at him affably.

"Are you hungry? Little brother, I invite you to eat watermelon. Watermelon can quench your thirst, and let you feel no more hungry."

"Thank you, but where is the watermelon?"

"This is the vine of a watermelon. You only need 顺藤摸瓜,[42] and you will be sure to get the melon." By saying that, the farmer left.

---

[41] 忍 rěn || jên \ bear; endure; tolerate. 饥[饑 or 飢] jī || chi \ be hungry; starve; famished. 挨 āi || ai \ suffer; endure. 饿[餓] è || ê \ hungry; starve. 忍饥挨饿: Endure hunger; bear starvation. (Idiom #41)

[42] 顺 shùn || shun \ along; in the same direction as. 藤 téng || t'êng \ vine. 摸 mō || mo \ grope for; feel for; feel; touch. 瓜 guā || kua \ melon. 顺藤摸瓜: Follow the vine to get the melon—solving a case by looking at the clues. (Idiom #42)

Following a thick vine Xiao Tao really got a big watermelon, and he was extremely happy.

Then he saw a sesame stalk by the roadway. Thinking of the sweet-smell of sesame seeds, he went to pick sesame seeds. He 捡了芝麻, 丢了西瓜.[43] The watermelon fell down on the ground and broke, and what Xiao Tao eventually got were merely two sesame seeds.

[43] 捡[撿] jiǎn || chien \ pick up; collect; gather. 了 le || lê \ <auxiliary word> (used after a verb to indicate the completion of an action) 芝麻 zhī má || chih ma \ sesame seed. 丢 diū || tiu \ lose; mislay. 西瓜 xī gua || hsi kua \ watermelon. 捡了芝麻, 丢了西瓜: Pick up the sesame seeds but overlook the watermelons; be frugal on small matters but wasteful on big ones—penny-wise clever but dollar-wise foolish. (Idiom #43)

§10

With Lips Gone, Teeth Felt Terribly Cold

Xiao Tao was tired and hungry again, but he continued to go eastward. When he found it was really hard to move because he was so tired, he sat under a tree to nap.

His teeth suddenly flied into a rage, saying that his lips were way too bad. "The lips take us as a back cushion everyday, and make us out of breath. We have never taken a vacation to admire the outside scenery."

The lips also complained about the teeth, "You chew thousands times everyday, and make us be terribly stressed. We have not had a holiday ever since you teeth's birth when Xiao Tao was an infant."

The lips blustered themselves into anger, and hid themselves at once. As soon as the teeth started to enjoy the scenic nature they got a severe cold. It was really 唇亡齿寒.[44]

Later, the lips appeared, but the teeth also angrily hid themselves. The lips were immediately flat and made a sunken mouth, just like a flat tire.

Xiao Tao mirrored his face at a nearby pond. Without the lips, his face showed a ferocious feature, just like a skull; and without the teeth, his face had only flattened lips, and he looked just like a 90-year old man.

---

[44] 唇 chún || ch'un \ lip. 亡 wáng || wang \ flee; be gone; die. 齿[齒] chǐ || ch'ih \ tooth. 寒 hán || han \ cold; tremble (with fear). 唇亡齿寒: If the lips are gone, the teeth will be cold; depend on one another; share a common fate. (Idiom #44)

"No! I can not be so ugly and old!" Xiao Tao said to his lips and teeth, "You should 唇齿相依,[45] and can not have internal conflict. Internal conflict will be no good to both of you guys!"

Lips and teeth felt that what Xiao Tao had said was right, and they 握手言欢.[46] They then all returned to their original posts.

Xiao Tao was glad to see his lips' and teeth's renewal of cordial relations.

Eventually he was woken up by his own shouts, and found that it was only a dream.

---

[45] 唇 chún || ch'un \ lip. 齿[齒] chǐ || ch'ih\ tooth. 相 xiāng || hsiang \ mutually; each other; one another. 依 yī || i \ depend on; rely on; comply with; be reluctant to part. 唇齿相依: Be closely related as lips and teeth; be mutually reliant; need each other. (Idiom #45)

[46] 握 wò || wo \ hold; grasp 手 shǒu || shou \ hand. 言 yán || yen \ speech; word. 欢[歡] huān || huan \ joyous; merry; jubilant. 握手言欢: Hold hands and chat cheerfully (to make up after a fight). (Idiom #46)

§11

At The Moment When a Heavyweight
Hanging by a Hair

At that time Xiao Tao smelled a smelly odor. Where did it come from? Xiao Tao lowered his head and tried to find it, and it was from the rotten duckweed in a pond. "流水不腐, 户枢不蠹,[47]" Xiao Tao remembered mom's teaching and thought: "一潭死水[48]will smell bad; and similarly, a man who does not use his brains will be foolish."

At the dead of night it was so dark that Xiao Tao could not see his hands in front of him. The chirrs of his cricket sounded aloud. But why were there hoofbeats?

Xiao Tao groped his way, by light of several lightning bugs around a pond he saw a man on horseback approaching the pond.

"It is so dark, what is he doing?" Before Xiao Tao thinking clearly the horse lost his footing and fell down, and more than half of the man's body stretched over of the edge of the pond.

---

[47] 流 liú || liu \ flow; drift. 水 shuǐ || shui \ water. 不 bù || pu \ no; not. 腐 fǔ || fu \ stale; rotten; corroded. 户 hù || hu \ door. 枢[樞] shū || shu \ pivot; hub; center. 蠹 dù || tu \ worm-eaten; moth-eaten; moth. 流水不腐, 户枢不蠹: Running water is never stale and a door hinge never gets worm-eaten—exercises keep one healthy; activity keeps one in shape. (Idiom #47)

[48] 一 yī || i \ one; single. 潭 tán || t'an \ deep pool; pond. 死 sǐ ||ssǔ \ dead; fixed; rigid. 水 shuǐ || shui \ water. 一潭死水: A pool of stagnant water—as still as death. (Idiom #48)

At the 千钧一发[49]time Xiao Tao promptly stretched his arms to hold the man's legs, hauled him away from the pond, and finally the man was out of danger.

The man said "thank you" repeatedly, and said that he was blind and the horse was blind too. How dangerous 盲人骑瞎马, 夜半临深池[50]was! Xiao Tao told the man not to 重蹈覆辙[51]thereafter. The man expressed that he would always bear in mind the lesson, "前事不忘, 后事之师."[52]

---

[49] 千 qiān || ch'ien \ thousand; a great amount of; a great number of. 钧[鈞] jūn || chün \ an ancient unit of weight (equal to 30 斤 [jīn || chin] or 33 pound). 一 yī || i \ one; single. 发[髮] fà || fa \ hair. 千钧一发: A heavyweight hanging by a hair—at a critical moment. (Idiom #49)

[50] 盲 máng || mang \ blind. 人 rén || jên \ person; people. 骑[騎] qí || ch'i \ ride (an animal or bicycle); sit on the back of. 瞎 xiā || hsia \ blind. 马[馬] mǎ || ma \ horse. 夜 yè || yeh \ night; evening. 半 bàn || pan \ half; in the middle; halfway. 临[臨] lín || lin \ face; arrive; just before. 深 shēn || shên \ deep. 池 chí || ch'ih \ pond; pool. 盲人骑瞎马, 夜半临深池: A blind man on a blind horse approaches a deep pond at midnight; head for danger—put one's head into the lion's mouth. (Idiom #50)

[51] 重 chóng || ch'ung \ repeat; again. 蹈 dǎo || tao \ tread; step. 覆 fù || fu \ overturn; upset. 辙[轍] zhé || chê \ the track of a wheel; rut. 重蹈覆辙: Follow the track of the overturned cart—make the same mistake again. (Idiom #51)

[52] 前 qián || ch'ien \ former; before; ago. 事 shì || shih \ matter; affair; thing. 不 bù || pu \ no; not. 忘 wàng || wang \ forget; overlook; neglect. 后[後] hòu || hou \ later; after; back; behind. 之 zhī || chih \ <auxiliary word> (used between an attribute and the word it modifies) 师[師] shī || shih \ teacher; guide; example. 前事不忘, 后事之师: Past experience, if not forgotton, can be guide for the future; learn from past mistakes. (Idiom #52)

§12

"Do Not Impose on Others
What You Yourself Do Not Desire"

For expressing his thanks the man took some food from his package and gave it to Xiao Tao.

Xiao Tao accepted it. He found the food was no other than chicken ribs. "This was 食之无味, 弃之可惜[53]stuff, and how could it be given as a gift?" Xiao Tao remembered that mom often said, "己所不欲, 勿施与人,"[54]but what the man had done was giving out the food he had not wanted.

However, Xiao Tao felt that many things might vary with each individual. The situation of a blind man was different from a healthy man.

---

[53] 食 shí || shih \ eat; food. 之 zhī || chih \ <pronoun> (used as an object) 无 [無] wú || wu \ not have; nothing; without. 味 wèi ||wei \ taste; flavor. 弃 [棄] qì || ch'i \ throw away; abandon; discard. 可 kě || k'ê \ can; may. 惜 xī || hsi \ have pity on; feel sorry for. 可惜: It's a pity. 食之无味, 弃之可惜: Hardly worth eating but not bad enough to throw away—in a state of dilemma; unsure what to do. (Idiom #53)

[54] 己 jǐ || chi \ oneself; one's own; personal. 所 suǒ || so \ <auxiliary word> (used before a verb to form a noun construction) what. 不 bù || pu \ don't; no; not. 欲 yù || yü \ desire; wish; want. 勿 wù || wu \ do not. 施 shī || shih \ exert; impose; grant. 于[於] yú || yü \ to; on; onto. 人 rén || jên \ people. 己所不欲, 勿施与人: Do not impose on others what you yourself do not desire—do onto others as you would have others done onto you. (Idiom #54)

He asked the blind man where the "chicken meat" came from, the man said he bought it from a grocery store.

Xiao Tao knew the boss of the grocery store, 老刁 (Lao Diao, lǎo diāo || lao tiao), and his nickname was "铁公鸡" (tiě gōng jī || t'ieh kung chi, "iron cock," from which no feather can be plucked—a stingy person; miser). "The 'iron cock' knew your eyes were no good, and gave you chicken ribs instead of chicken meat. He 欺人太甚. [55]Tomorrow early morning I will help you to reason with the guy!"

"Let it be, let it be. 得饶人处且饶人,[56]We do not need 斤斤计较,"[57]said the blind man.

Xiao Tao agreed with what the blind man had said, and made friends with him. They talked a long time by the pond. Later, the blind man wanted to go home. Xiao Tao helped him to get on the horseback. They shook hands and said goodbye.

---

[55] 欺 qī || ch'i \ deceive; bully; take advantage of. 人 rén || jên \ people. 太 tài || t'ai \ excessively; too; over. 甚 shèn || shên \ very; extremely. 太甚: too far; to the extreme. 欺人太甚: Bully others too much; intimidate others too much. (Idiom #55)

[56] 得 dé || tê \ can (or may).饶[饒] ráo || jao \ forgive; pardon; have mercy on. 人 rén || jên \ people. 处[處] chù || ch'u \ place; point; part. 且 qiě || ch'ieh \ just; for the time being. 得饶人处且饶人: Forgive the others when one can; forgive others; let things pass. (Idiom #56)

[57] 斤 jīn || ch'in \ a unit of weight (= 0.5 kilogram or 1.1 pound). 计[計] jì || chi \ count; compute; calculate. 较[較] jiào || chiao \ compare; dispute. 计较: haggle over; fuss about; argue; dispute. 斤斤计较: Dispute over every ounce; stingy; miserly; tightfisted. (Idiom #57)

§13

Xiao Tao Cut His Feet to Fit His Shoes

Xiao Tao resumed his journey, although he was pretty tired.

Unfortunately, he got blisters on his feet, and had difficulty in taking every step. The good thing was, a group of lightning bugs flew around and made something on the ground seeable.

He touched a lustrous thing and soon the thing burst out: "I am a 削铁如泥[58]precious knife!" Xiao Tao hurried to grasp the handle of the knife, and was happy for a while.

The foot pain made him hobble. He did not know his feet were swollen until he took off his shoes. He then wanted to wear his shoes back on his feet but they were too tight. He was so anxious that he looked like 热锅上的蚂蚁[59]running round and round.

He became so mad that he used his knife to "treat" his feet, 削足适履,[60]and before long blood streamed down. He felt so painful and he was so grieved as to wish he were dead. He tore his clothes to strips to bind

---

[58] 削 **xuē** || **hsüeh** \ cut; whittle; pare. 铁[鐵] **tiě** || **t'ieh** \ iron. 如 **rú** || **ju** \ like; as; as if. 泥 **ní** || **ni** \ mud. 削铁如泥: Cut through iron as if it were mud; sharp; quick (usually describes a knife). (Idiom #58)

[59] 热[熱] **rè** || **jê** \ hot; heat; warm. 锅[鍋] **guō** || **kuo** \ pot; pan; boiler. 上 **shàng** || **shang** \ on top of; on the surface of; above; over. 的 **de** || **tê** \ <auxiliary word> (used after an attribute). 蚂蚁 [螞蟻] **mǎ yǐ** || **ma i** \ ant. 热锅上的蚂蚁: An ant on a hot pan—agitated; perturbed. (Idiom #59)

[60] 削 **xuē** || **hsüeh** \ cut; pare. 足 **zú** || **tsu** \ foot. 适[適] **shì** || **shih** \ fit; suitable; proper. 履 **lǚ** || **lü** \ shoe. 削足适履: Cut the feet to fit the shoes—willing to sacrifice oneself in order to achieve a small goal. (Idiom #60)

up his wounds without losing time, and then waited for a long time for the blood to stop.

He took a pair of straw sandals out from his parcel and put his shoes into the parcel. He wore the sandals and tried to walk haltingly by means of two branches used as sticks for support.

Cutting the feet to fit the shoes was an absurd action. No wonder this section is numbered thirteen. (Like the western countries' *thirteen superstition*, in China, thirteen is also an unlucky number. For instance, in Shanghai, "13 points" means "crazy" or "silly.")

§14

Xiao Tao Warned the Queen Ant

Xiao Tao continued to hobble eastwards. The road became narrower and narrower, and he came to a dead end.

The sky was turning bright in the east and another day was breaking. He saw a great mass of ants in a line crawling westwards, with each carrying a piece of dirt on the back. They were constructing their nest in a dyke.

千里之堤, 溃于蚁穴.[61] This was terribly dangerous! Xiao Tao dissuaded these ants at once, but all the worker ants 装聋作哑[62] and took no heed of what he had said.

---

[61] 千 qiān || ch'ien \ thousand; a great amount of; a great number of. 里 lǐ || li \ a Chinese unit of length (= 0.5 kilometer =~ 0.31 mile). 之 zhī || chih \ <auxiliary word> (used to connect the modifier and the word it modifies) 堤 dī || ti \ dyke; embankment. 溃[潰] kuì || k'uei \ (of a dyke or dam) burst; break through (an encirclement). 于 yú || yü \ at; in. 蚁[蟻] yǐ || i \ ant. 穴 xué || hsüeh \ hole; cave; den. 千里之堤, 溃于蚁穴: One ant-hole may cause the collapse of a thousand *li* long dyke—a small problem that is not fixed can lead to a greater problem. (Idiom #61)

[62] 装[裝] zhuāng || chuang \ pretend; feign. 聋[聾] lóng || lung \ deaf. 作 zuò || tso \ pretend; affect. 哑[啞] yǎ || ya \ mute; dumb. 装聋作哑: Pretend to be deaf and mute; pretend to be ignorant. (Idiom #62)

Xiao Tao thought 擒贼先擒王,[63]and went to warn the queen ant who was sitting in an imperial sedan. "If the dyke collapses, the entire Kingdom of Ants will 葬身鱼腹!"[64]

The queen ant was frightened, and she ordered to build their nest somewhere else.

---

[63] 擒 qín || ch'in \ capture; catch; seize. 贼[賊] zéi || tsei \ thief; brigand. 先 xiān || hsien \ first; at first; in advance. 王 wáng || wang \ king; monarch. 擒贼先擒王: To catch brigands, first catch their king (i.e. the ringleader)—to eliminate the heart of the problem. (Idiom #63)

[64] 葬 zàng || tsang \ bury. 身 shēn || shên \ body. 鱼[魚] yú || yü \ fish. 腹 fù || fu \ belly; abdomen; stomach. 葬身鱼腹: Be buried in the stomachs of fishes; becomes food for the fishes—drowned. (Idiom #64)

§15

Xiao Tao Met a Great Master of Painting

Along the dyke Xiao Tao hobbled northwards, but soon he felt every direction was the same "bleak and desolate." Seeing the wild scenery, Xiao Tao felt a sense of puzzlement, since he did not know where to go.

A line of geese hovered over Xiao Tao's head with loud quacks. He raised his head a little and saw a big road on the horizon. It was really 山穷水尽疑无路, 柳暗花明又一村.[65]Xiao Tao was very happy and went towards it. The road led him into a village.

This was a beautiful mountain village, and there were many industrious and valiant villagers.

Xiao Tao saw a gentleman, Painter 张 (Zhang, zhāng || chang) was painting on a wall. He painted a 张牙舞爪[66]dragon, but he didn't draw the eyeballs in the eyes.

Xiao Tao said, "You forgot to draw the eyeballs."

---

[65] 山 shān || shan \ hill; mountain. 穷[窮] qióng || ch'iung \ end; limit; poor. 水 shuǐ || shui \ water; a general term for rivers, lakes, seas, etc. 尽[盡] jìn || chin \ exhausted; finished; to the limit. 疑 yí || i \ doubt; suspect; doubtful. 无[無] wú || wu \ nothing; there is not. 路 lù || lu \ road; path; way. 柳 liǔ || liu \ willow. 暗 àn || an \ dark; dim; dull. 花 huā || hua \ flower. 明 míng || ming \ bright, brilliant, light. 又 yòu || yu \ again; also. 一 yī || i \ one. 村 cūn || ts'un \ village. 山穷水尽疑无路, 柳暗花明又一村: Where the hills and streams end and there seems no road beyond, amidst shading willows and blooming flowers another village appears—have renewed hope in a seemingly desperate situation. (Idiom #65)

[66] 张[張] zhāng || chang \ open; spread; stretch. 牙 yá || ya \ tooth, fang. 舞 wǔ || wu \ wield; brandish; flourish; dance. 爪 zhǎo || chao \ claw; paw.

Painter Zhang said, "If I put eyeballs into the eyes, the dragon will fly away."

"I do not believe, and I can not believe!"

The painter then started to draw the eyeballs. As soon as he finished painting the eyeballs, with a rumble, the dragon really flew away, and left behind a big hole on the wall.

Xiao Tao was 目瞪口呆.[67] In this world 画龙点睛[68] really happened!

张牙舞爪: Bare fangs and brandish claws—have a frightening demeanor; frightening like a beast. (Idiom #66)

[67] 目 mù || mu \ eye. 瞪 dèng || têng \ open (one's eyes) wide; stare; glare. 口 kǒu || k'ou \ mouth; opening. 呆 dāi || tai \ slow-witted; dull. 目瞪口呆: Be struck dumb; dumbstruck; be stunned; be shocked. (Idiom #67)

[68] 画[畫] huà || hua \ draw; paint; drawing; picture. 龙[龍] lóng || lung \ dragon; imperial. 点[點] diǎn || tien \ dot stroke; spot. 睛 jīng || ching \ eyeball, pupil. 画龙点睛: Bring a picture of a dragon to life by putting in the eyeballs (or pupils) of its eyes—to bring home a point (usually in a painting, in literature on in a conversation). (Idiom #68)

§16

Xiao Tao Drew a Snake and Added Feet to It

After a while Xiao Tao asked the painter: "Is there something magical in your painting brush?"

"No."

"Then why could the dragon fly away? May I borrow your brush to draw some pictures?"

"Sure you can," nodded the painter, and handed Xiao Tao the brush.

"What do I want to draw?" Xiao Tao thought while spreading the drawing paper. "Well, as the old saying 龙腾虎跃[69]goes, now that he already drew a dragon, let me draw a tiger!"

Xiao Tao started the tiger drawing. He 抓耳挠腮[70]for a while before taking up the painting brush, and then 一气呵成[71]a tiger.

Painter Zhang asked, "What did you draw?"

"Can't you recognize it?" Xiao Tao was a little upset. "I have drawn a tiger."

---

[69] 龙[龍] lóng || lung \ dragon. 腾[騰]téng || t'èng \ rise; soar; jump. 虎 hǔ || hu \ tiger. 跃 [躍]yuè || yüeh \ leap; jump. 龙腾虎跃: Dragons rising and tigers leaping—a scene full of life. (Idiom #69)

[70] 抓 zhuā || chua \ grab; seize; tweak; catch. 耳 ěr || êrh \ ear. 挠[撓] náo || nao \ scratch. 腮 sāi || sai \ cheek. 抓耳挠腮: Tweak one's ears and scratch one's cheeks (when one is deep in thought). (Idiom #70)

[71] 一 yī || i \ once; one; single; alone; only one. 气[氣] qì ||ch'i \ breath; gas; air. 呵 hē || hê \ exhale (with one's mouth open). 成 chéng || ch'êng \ accomplish; succeed; achievement. 一气呵成: Get something done at one go; fulfill a task without pause. (Idiom #71)

"It seems to me not a tiger," the painter shook his head repeatedly, "It is like a dog. You did 画虎类犬,[72]" laughed while he talked.

Xiao Tao 面红耳赤[73]said, "I am not a painter, but I can also draw a snake. Let my snake mix with your dragon, and this is called 龙蛇混杂.[74]"

"OK, you draw a snake, please!"

Actually Xiao Tao had never seen a snake before. "How does a snake look like?" He thought over and again, and remembered that dad once had been bitten by a snake, and he was afraid of ropes since then. Mom laughed at dad, "You 一朝被蛇咬, 十年怕井绳.[75]Therefore a snake was just like a coiled rope.

Based on his cleverness Xiao Tao drew a snake, which coiled its body, opened its mouth and stretched out its tongue.

"Your drawing is not bad," said Painter Zhang.

Just after Painter Zhang nodded his head and praised the drawing, with one stroke of the painting brush Xiao Tao drew feet under the body of the snakes. He added four feet for the snake.

---

[72] 画[畫] huà || hua \ draw; paint; drawing. 虎 hǔ || hu \ tiger. 类[類] lèi || lei \ resemble. 犬 quǎn || ch'üan \ dog. 画虎类犬: Try to draw a tiger and end up with the likeness of a dog—take on a task that exceeds one's ability and result in failure. (Idiom #72)

[73] 面 miàn || mien \ face. 红[紅] hóng || hung \ red; flush. 耳 ěr || êrh \ ear. 赤 chì || ch'ih \ red; bare. 面红耳赤: Be red in the face; blushed (in embarrassment). (Idiom #73)

[74] 龙[龍] lóng || lung \ dragon. 蛇 shé || shě \ snake; serpent. 混 hùn || hun \ jumble; mix. 杂[雜] zá || tsa \ mixed; jumbled; miscellaneous. 龙蛇混杂: Dragons and snakes jumbled together—bad people mixed in with the good people (Idiom #74)

[75] 一 yī || i \ one. 朝 zhāo || chao \ day. 被 bèi || pei \ <auxiliary word> (used in a passive sentence before a noun to introduce the doer of the action) 蛇 shé || shě \ snake; serpent. 咬 yǎo || yao \ bite. 十 shí || shih \ ten. 年 nián || nien \ year. 怕 pà || p'a \ fear; be afraid of. 井 jǐng || ching \ well. 绳[繩] shéng || shêng \ rope; cord; string. 一朝被蛇咬, 十年怕井绳: Once bit by a snake, one shies at coiled rope for ten years—once bit, twice shy. (Idiom #75)

Painter Zhang then shook his head again and again. "A snake has no feet at all, but you 画蛇添足.[76] You made an unnecessary move."

---

[76] 画[畫] huà || hua \ draw; paint; drawing; picture. 蛇 shé || shê \ snake; serpent. 添 tiān || t'ien \ add; increase. 足 zú || tsu \ foot. 画蛇添足: Draw a snake and then add feet to it—do something unnecessary and get negative effect. (Idiom #76)

§17

The Dragon Fan Actually Feared Dragons

In the village there was an old pedant by the last name of 叶(Ye, yè || yeh) Lord Ye, a hoary-headed short man, was engaged in the research of dragons all his life, and was fond of dragons.

In Lord Ye's house, there were many painted wooden dragons on trusses and pillars. He hung dragons' portraits on walls, enshrined porcelain and pottery clay dragons in his shrine, and paid homage to dragons everyday. He even let his bedstead to be wrapped by dragons—of course they were made of wood.

Dragons in heaven were deeply touched. They flew down and entered Lord Ye's yard. One dragon popped his head into a window and said hello to Ye.

叶公好龙,[77] actually, he only loved fake dragons. When real dragons came he was frightened out of his wits, 面如土色,[78] and eventually 溜之大吉.[79]

---

[77] 叶[葉] yè || yeh [In old times it was pronounced as "shê || shè."] \ Ye (a surname). 公 gōng || kung \ (a respectful term of address for an elderly man). 好 hào || hao \ like; love; be fond of. 龙[龍] lóng || lung \ dragon. 叶公好龙: Lord Ye's love of dragons—to claim a liking for something which one actually fears. (Idiom #77)

[78] 面 miàn || mien \ face. 如 rú || ju \ like; as; as if. 土 tǔ || t'u \ soil; earth. 色 sè || sê \ color; look. 面如土色: Look pasty; look pallid. (Idiom #78)

[79] 溜 liū || liu \ sneak off; slip away; escape. 之 zhī || chih \ <auxiliary word> 大 dà || ta \ in a big way; big; large; great. 吉 jí || chi \ lucky. 大吉 (used ironically) very lucky. 溜之大吉: Sneak away; run away (usually from responsibility). (Idiom #79)

§18

Ah Er Plugged His Ears while Stealing a Bell

Lord Ye was a well-known rich man in the locality. After his leaving home, his neighbor 阿二 (Ah Er, ā èr || a êrh), a thin man with the head of a buck and the eyes of a rat, thought an evil idea—to steal Lord Ye's property.

One night Ah Er climbed over a wall and entered Lord Ye's yard. A bell connected to the door rang after his forcing open the locked door, and made him be in a cold sweat.

"What to do?" Ah Er thought for a long time, and decided to steal the bell altogether to avoid trouble. "The bell was made by excellent workmanship and could be sold for a good price," he thought.

For preventing the bell from stirring up trouble, Ah Er used his hands to tightly cover his ears. He bit on the string that had fastened the bell to the door. The bell rang again but Ah Er did not hear anything at all. He succeeded in 掩耳盗铃.[80] Ah Er felt lucky because nobody was there.

However, 隔墙有耳,[81] Xiao Tao was right outside the wall. Xiao Tao could shout to stop Ar Er, but he wanted to see what the thief

---

[80] 掩 yǎn || yen \ cover; shut; close. 耳 ěr || êrh \ ear. 盗 dào || tao \ steal; rob. 铃[鈴] líng || ling \ bell. 掩耳盗铃: Plug one's ears while stealing a bell—to lie to oneself; be an ostrich with his head in the sand; the cat closes his eyes when stealing cream. (Idiom #80)

[81] 隔 gé || kê \ separate; cut off; at a distance from. 墙[牆] qiáng || ch'iang \ wall. 有 yǒu || yu \ have; there is; exist. 耳 ěr || êrh \ ear. 隔墙有耳: The walls have ears. (Idiom #81)

would do the next. For avoiding 打草惊蛇,[82]he just held his breath in concentration.

Ah Er wrapped up the bell with a piece of cloth, and passed through the hall into the inner chamber. He 翻箱倒柜[83]to search for treasures. But he saw only dragons in paintings or made of soil.

Ah Er searched from living room to study, and from bedroom to latrine, and then from kitchen to dining room. In addition to dragons in paintings and made of soil, he saw paper dragons. Ah Er had no interest in dragons, and resigned himself to his bad luck.

There was spirit in a wine cellar. Ah Er was a drunkard. He held a wine jug and drank wolfishly. He tipsily went to the bedroom to sleep,

---

[82] 打 **dǎ** || **ta** \ beat; strike; hit; attack. 草 **cǎo** || **ts'ao** \ grass; straw. 惊[驚] **jīng** || **ching** \ startle; surprise; shock; alarm. 蛇 **shé** || **shê** \ snake; serpent. 打草惊蛇: Beat the grass and startle the snake—make noise and alert the culprit. (Idiom #82)

[83] 翻 **fān** || **fan** \ turn over; rummage; search. 箱 **xiāng** || **hsiang** \ chest; case; trunk. 倒 **dǎo** || **tao** \ turn upside down; topple. 柜[櫃] **guì** || **kuei** \ cupboard; cabinet. 翻箱倒柜: Rummage through boxes and chests; search thoroughly and make a mess. (Idiom #83)

IDIOM #80

but he felt everything was reeling before his eyes. He fell down, and his hip sat on uneven floor.

"Why is the floor uneven?" He stretched his hands to touch the floor, lifted several clinker tiles, and he found that underneath were gleaming silver 元宝! (yuán bǎo || yüan pao: a shoe-shaped silver or gold ingot used as money in feudal China)

踏破铁鞋无觅处，得来全不费工夫.[84] "人为财死，鸟为食亡.[85] Heaven helps me!" Ah Er 欣喜若狂.[86] He counted the silver ingots again and again, and found it was 300 taels. He would not worry about money for the rest of his life!

Using the quilt on the bed he wrapped the silver ingots. For the stolen bell, he just disregarded it. He buried the wine jug and the bell in the former silver ingot hole, and covered the hole with the clinker tiles. He left no evidence of the crime, just like 天衣无缝.[87]

---

[84]   踏 tà || t'a \ step on; tread. 破 pò || p'o \ broken; damaged; worn-out. 铁[鐵] tiě || t'ieh \ iron. 鞋 xié || hsieh \ shoes. 无[無] wú || wu \ not have; there is not. 觅 mì || mi \ look for; hunt for; seek. 处[處] chù || ch'u \ place. 得 dé || tê \ get, obtain, gain. 来[來] lái || lai \ (used after a verb indicating completeness) 得来 (indicating capability or possibility to get) 全 quán || ch'üan \ entirely; completely. 不 bù || pu \ no; not. 费[費] fèi || fei \ cost; spend. 工 gōng || kung \ work; labor. 夫 fū || fu \ man. 工夫: effort; work; time. 踏破铁鞋无觅处，得来全不费工夫: One can wear out iron shoes in fruitless searching, and yet by a lucky chance he may find the thing without even looking for it; spend much time in futile search, yet find what one is looking for by sheer luck. (Idiom #84)

[85]   人 rén || jên \ person; people. 为[為] wèi || wei \ for. 财[財] cái || ts'ai \ wealth; money. 死 sǐ || ssŭ \ die; decease. 鸟[鳥] niǎo || niao \ bird. 食 shí || shih \ eat; meal; food. 亡 wáng || wang \ die. 人为财死，鸟为食亡: Men will die for wealth, as birds will for food—man is greedy. (Idiom #85)

[86]   欣 xīn || hsin \ glad; happy; joyful. 喜 xǐ || hsi \ happy; delighted; pleased. 若 ruò || jo \ like; seem; as if. 狂 kuáng || k'uang \ mad; crazy. 欣喜若狂: Be ecstatic; extremely happy. (Idiom #86)

[87]   天 tiān || t'ien \ sky; heaven. 衣 yī || i \ clothing; clothes; garment. 无 wú || wu \ not have; there is not; without. 缝[縫] fèng || fêng \ seam; crack; fissure. 天衣无缝: A seamless heavenly robe—perfect; faultless. (Idiom #87)

55

He wanted to go out, but still felt uncomfortable. This was perhaps 做贼心虚.[88]

Ah Er talked to himself, "Lord Ye saw me several times when I peeked into his home through the hole on the wall, and he will suspect me." For getting rid of the suspicion, he used a painting brush to write crookedly two lines on a piece of paper:

此地无银三百两,
隔壁阿二不曾偷.[89]

Ah Er 自作聪明,[90]when leaving he did not forget to padlock the door.

若要人不知, 除非己莫为.[91]Lord Ye saw what Ah Er had written on the paper after returning home, looked at the site for the silver ingots and was sure that Ah Er was the thief. He then took the paper, and went

---

[88] 做 zuò || tso \ be; become; do; act; make. 贼[賊] zéi || tsei \ thief; burglar. 心 xīn || hsin \ heart; feeling. 虚 xū || hsü \ timid; diffident; empty; void; in vain. 做贼心虚: As a thief is afraid of being found out; be ill at ease; have troubled conscience. (Idiom #88)

[89] 此 cǐ || ts'ǔ\ this. 地 dì || ti \ place; land; ground. 无[無] wú || wu \ not have; there is not. 银[銀] yín || yin \ silver. 三 sān || san \ three. 百 bǎi || pai \ hundred. 两[兩] liǎng || liang \ tael (1 liang = 1 tael = 31.25 grams = 1.102 ounce). 隔 gé || kê \ separate; cut off; at a distance from. 壁 bì || pi \ wall. 隔壁: next door. 不 bù || pu \ no; not. 曾 céng || ts'êng \ once; at one time. 偷 tōu || t'ou \ steal; burglarize. 此地无银三百两, 隔壁阿二不曾偷: No 300 taels of silver buried here, and next-door Ah Er did not steal—make a denial that leads to self-incrimination. (Idiom #89)

[90] 自 zì || tsǔ\ self; oneself; one's own. 作 zuò || tso \ regard as; feel; act as. 聪[聰] cōng || ts'ung \ faculty of hearing; acute hearing. 明 míng || ming \ bright, brilliant, sharp-eyed; understand, know. 聪明 intelligent; bright; clever. 自作聪明: Regard oneself as very clever (Idiom #90)

[91] 若 ruò || jo \ if. 要 yào || yao \ want; wish; desire. 人 rén || jên \ people. 不 bù || pu \ no; not. 知 zhī || chih \ know; realize; be aware of. 除 chú || ch'u \ except; besides; get rid of. 非 fēi || fei \ not; no. 除非: only if; only when; unless. 己 jǐ || chi \ oneself; one's own; personal. 莫 mò || mo \ don't; no; not. 为[為] wéi || wei \ do; act. 若要人不知, 除非己莫为: If you don't

56

to the county government to report the case by beating a drum in front of the gate of the governmental building.

The county magistrate ordered the detention of the suspect Ah Er.

---

want anyone to know what you have done, it is better not to have done it in the first place. (Idiom #91)

§19

Ah Er Felt as if His Eyebrows Were Burning

Seeing that people were chasing him, Ah Er felt 火烧眉毛,[92]but he 情急智生.[93]He hid the parcel in a dark corner of a nearby household yard, and started to 贼喊捉贼.[94]This really worked. A policeman asked him where was the thief, and he pointed to a young man afar. When policemen were chasing the young man, Ah Er turned to the other direction and ran away.

However, people's eyes were discerning. Xiao Tao had heard the bell ringing and had seen Ah Er behaving stealthily like a thief, guessed he was not a good man, and followed him 如影随形.[95]

---

[92] 火 huǒ || huo \ fire. 烧[燒] shāo || shao \ burn. 眉 méi || mei \ eyebrow. 毛 máo || mao \ hair. 眉毛: eyebrow; brow. 火烧眉毛: The fire is singeing the eyebrows—an urgent situation; a critical matter. (Idiom #92)

[93] 情 qíng || ch'ing \ situation; circumstances; condition. 急 jí || chi \ urgent; pressing; urgency; emergency. 智 zhì || chih \ wisdom; wit. 生 shēng || shêng \ give birth to; bear; come into existence. 情急智生: Have a good idea in a desperate situation. (Idiom #93)

[94] 贼[賊] zéi || tsei \ thief; burglar. 喊: hǎn || han \ shout; cry out; yell. 捉 zhuō || cho \ catch; capture; grasp. 贼喊捉贼: A thief shouting "Stop thief!"—to dodge responsibility. (Idiom #94)

[95] 如 rú || ju \ like; as; as if. 影 yǐng || ying \ shadow; reflection; image. 随[隨] suí || sui \ to follow. 形 xíng || hsing \ body; form; shape; appearance. 如影随形: Like a shadow always follows one. (Idiom #95)

Ah Er was a single man, and had no relative, and therefore had no place to hide. He was caught in a 倾盆大雨,[96] and looked like a drenched chicken.

Xiao Tao was also soaked through, fortunately he wore a cap at that time. He pounced on Ah Er. Ah Er was greatly astonished. But he saw Xiao Tao was only a child, and therefore was not afraid of him.

Ah Er said to Xiao Tao, "Child, you and I 井水不犯河水.[97] Why do you attack me?"

Xiao Tao responded to him, "Everyone has the responsibility to capture a thief!"

---

[96] 倾 qīng || ch'ing \ overturn and pour out; empty. 盆 pén || p'ên \ basin; tub. 大 dà || ta \ big; heavy. 雨 yǔ || yü \ rain. 倾盆大雨: Downpour; rain cats and dogs. (Idiom #96)

[97] 井 jǐng || ching \ well. 水 shuǐ || shui \ water. 不 bù || pu \ no; not. 犯 fàn || fan \ violate; intrude; assail. 河 hé || hê \ river. 井水不犯河水: Well water does not intrude into river water—minding one's own business. (Idiom #97)

§20

Xiao Tao Was So Angry That His Hairs Sprang up and Lifted His Cap

Ah Er 狗急跳墙,[98]and slapped Xiao Tao's face. Xiao Tao 怒发冲冠,[99]and his five hairs became five springs perpendicular to his scalp. He kicked Ah Er. The two wrestled. Unfortunately, Xiao Tao was too weak to beat Ah Er, and gradually lost, and Ah Er's fists made Xiao Tao's nose bleed.

At that time people 蜂拥而来,[100]but most of them only 袖手旁观.[101]

---

[98] 狗 gǒu || kou \ dog. 急 jí || chi \ urgent; pressing; urgency; emergency. 跳 tiào || t'iao \ jump. 墙[牆] qiáng || ch'iang \ wall. 狗急跳墙: A cornered dog might jump over the wall—desperate person might do something irrational. (Idiom #98)

[99] 怒 nù || nu \ anger; rage; fury. 发[髮] fà || fa \ hair. 冲[沖 or 衝] chōng || ch'ung \ charge; rush; dash. 冠 guān || kuan \ hat. 怒发冲冠: One's angry hairs spring up and lift one's hat—be irate; outraged; infuriated. (Idiom #99)

[100] 蜂 fēng || fêng \ wasp; bee. 拥[擁] yōng || yung \ crowd; throng; swarm; gather around. 而 ér || êrh \ <conjunction> (connecting an adverbial element to a verb) 来[來]lái || lai \ come; arrive. 蜂拥而来:Come forward like a swarm. (Idiom #100)

[101] 袖 xiù || hsiu \ sleeve. 手 shǒu || shou \ hand. 旁 páng || p'ang \ side. 观[觀] guān || kuan \ look at; watch; observe. 袖手旁观: Look on with folded arms; be bystanders; look on without getting involved. (Idiom #101)

Among the people one with heavy features 路见不平, 拔刀相助,[102]and promptly caught Ah Er.

---

[102] 路 lù || lu \ road; path; way. 见[見] jiàn || chien \ see; catch sight of. 不 bù || pu \ no; not. 平 píng || p'ing \ fair; impartial; even. 不平: injustice; unfairness; wrong; grievance. 拔 bá || pa \ pull out; pull up. 刀 dāo || tao \ knife; sword. 相 xiāng || hsiang \ (indicating an action performed by one person toward another) 助 zhù || chu \ help; assist; aid. 路见不平, 拔刀相助: See injustice on the road and draw one's knife to help the victim—come to the aid of one who has been unjustly treated. (Idiom #102)

§21

A Rat Running across the Street, with Everybody Shouting, "Kill It!"

Xiao Tao told the one with heavy features, "He is a thief."
老鼠过街,人人喊打.[103]People 异口同声[104]said that the thief should be severely punished.

Ah Er was sent under escort to a local authority. Xiao Tao also went there.

In the local authority there was a horizontal inscribed board with the inscription of "明镜高悬."[105]The county magistrate ordered to bring the suspect to the court.

---

[103] 老 **lǎo** || lao \ <used as a prefix> (in certain names of animals)鼠 **shǔ** || shu \ mouse; rat. 老鼠: mouse; rat. 过[過] **guò** || kuo \ cross; pass; across; past; through. 街 **jiē** || chieh \ street. 人 **rén** || jên \ man; person; people. 人人: everybody; everyone. 喊 **hǎn** || han \ shout; cry out; yell. 打 **dǎ** || ta \ strike; beat; hit; knock. 老鼠过街, 人人喊打: A rat running across the street, with everybody shouting, "Kill it!" (Usually describes a public enemy) (Idiom #103)

[104] 异[異] **yì** || i \ different. 口 **kǒu** || k'ou \ mouth. 同 **tóng** || t'ung \ same; alike; in common. 声[聲] **shēng** || shêng \ sound; voice. 异口同声: With one voice; in complete unison. (Idiom #104)

[105] 明 **míng** || ming \ clear; bright, light. 镜[鏡] **jìng** || ching \ looking glass; mirror. 高 **gāo** || kao \ tall; high. 悬[懸] **xuán** || hsüan \ hang; suspend. 明镜高悬: A clear mirror hung on high (generally used to describe an honest, impartial and wise official or judge). (Idiom #105)

Ah Er cried loudly about the "injustice." The magistrate showed Ah Er the paper on which he had written "此地无银三百两, 隔壁阿二不曾偷," but Ah Er 矢口否认,[106]and said he was illiterate and did not understand what the writing meant at all. Of course, he said he had never written the two-line note.

The county magistrate struck a 惊堂木 (a wooden block used by a magistrate to strike the table in calling for attention or order), and said, "Pretending to be naïve or stupid will be punished further."

Ah Er went on denying, and 反咬一口[107]Xiao Tao. Ah Er said that he had seen Xiao Tao digging for the silver ingots so hard that it caused a nosebleed, and he had tried to capture the young thief.

Although Ah Er's testimony 牛头不对马嘴,[108]the magistrate did not want to overlook any 蛛丝马迹.[109]Now there were two suspects. The magistrate had to detain the two temporarily, and dispatch a criminal policeman to investigate the case until 水落石出.[110]

---

[106] 矢 shǐ || shih \ vow; swear; arrow. 口 kǒu || k'ou \ mouth. 矢口: insist stressfully. 否 fǒu || fou \ negate; deny; no. 认[認] rèn || jên \ recognize; know; admit. 矢口否认: Firmly deny. (Idiom #106)

[107] 反 fǎn || fan \ turn over; in an opposite direction; in reverse. 咬 yǎo || yao \ bite; snap at. 一 yī || i \ one. 口 kǒu || k'ou \ mouth. 反咬一口: Bite back—make a phony countercharge against one's accuser. (Idiom #107)

[108] 牛 niú || niu \ ox; cow; bull. 头[頭] tóu || t'ou \ head. 不 bù || pu \ no; not. 对[對] duì || lui \ fit one into the other, suit, agree. 马[馬] mǎ || ma \ horse. 嘴 zuǐ || tsui \ mouth. 牛头不对马嘴: Horses' jaws don't match cow's heads—unsuitable, conflicting. (Idiom #108)

[109] 蛛 zhū || chu \ spider. 丝[絲] sī || ssǔ\ a threadlike thing; silk; trace. 马[馬] mǎ || ma \ horse. 迹[跡] jī || chi \ mark; trace; remains. 蛛丝马迹: The thread of a spider and the trail of a horse—clues or evidence. (Idiom #109)

[110] 水 shuǐ || shui \ water. 落 luò || lo \ fall; drop; go down; sink. 石 shí || shih \ stone; rock. 出 chū || ch'u \ go or come out; emerge; appear. 水落石出: when the water subsides the rocks emerge—get to the bottom of the whole thing. (Idiom #110)

Ah Er was a 好吃懒做[111]and 不务正业[112]rogue. He always had unpaid bills but never paid them back. The policeman brought many 白条 (bái tiáo || pai t' iao \ promissory notes with little binding force) which Ah Er had given to restaurants and groceries. After court secretary's identifying the handwriting, Ah Er was confirmed to be the criminal of the case. Then the court session began.

In the court session, Ah Er went on denying any fault. He accused the official of "欲加之罪, 何患无词."[113]However, Ah Er actually 欲盖弥彰,[114]because an illiterate man could hardly use 文质彬彬[115] words such as "欲加之罪, 何患无词."

---

[111] 好 hào || hao \ like; love; be fond of. 吃 chī || ch'ih \ eat; take. 懒 lǎn || lan \ lazy. 做 zuò || tso \ do; make; produce. 好吃懒做: Be greedy for food and lazy at work; be gluttonous and slothful. (Idiom #111)

[112] 不 bù || pu \ no; not. 务[務] wù || wu \ be engaged in; devote one's efforts to. 正 zhèng || chêng \ honest; correct; right. 业[業] yè || yeh \ line of business; trade; job. 不务正业: Do not have decent job; have no honest profession. (Idiom #112)

[113] 欲 yù || yü \ desire; wish; want. 加 jiā || chia \ add; give; put in. 之 zhī || chih \ <auxiliary word> (used to connect the modifier and the word it modifies) 罪 zuì || tsui \ crime; guilt; blame. 何 hé || hê \ what; why. 患 huàn || huan \ anxiety; worry. 无[無] wú || wu \ not have; there is not; nothing. 词[詞] cí || ts'ǔ \ statement; word. 欲加之罪,何患无词: If one intends to condemn somebody, he will easily make up a false charge—he who has a mind to beat his dog will easily find his stick. (Idiom #113)

[114] 欲 yù || yü \ desire; wish; want. 盖[蓋] gài || kai \ put a cover on; cover; lid. 弥[彌] mí || mi \ more; even more. 彰 zhāng || chang \ clear; evident; make known. 欲盖弥彰: The more one tries to cover up a wrong doing, the more obvious it becomes; try to hide something, only to make it more exposed. (Idiom #114)

[115] 文 wén || wên \ gentle, refined; culture; civilian. 质[質] zhì || chih \ nature; character; quality. 彬 bīn || pin \ cultivated; well-bred. 彬彬: <formal> refined. 文质彬彬: Polite; well-mannered. (Idiom #115)

Ah Er was a 不见棺材不落泪[116]fellow. In front of 白纸黑字, 铁证如山,[117]he had to plead guilty. However, he still quibbled, and said: "I was an honest man. If I had not drunk so much hard liquor, I would have not got into this trouble."

[116] 不 bù || pu \ no; not. 见 jiàn || chien \ see; catch sight of. 棺 guān || kuan \ coffin. 材 cái || ts'ai \ timber; material; coffin. 棺材: coffin. 落 luò || lo \ fall; drop. 泪 [淚] lèi || lei \ tear; teardrop. 落泪 \: shed tears; weep. 不见棺材不落泪: Not shed tears until one sees his coffin—ignore the truth until confronted with it. (Idiom #116)

[117] 白 bái || pai \ white; plain; blank. 纸[紙] zhǐ || chih \ paper. 黑 hēi || hei \ black; dark. 字 zì || tsǔ \ word; character; writings. 铁[鐵] tiě || t'ieh \ indisputable; unalterable; iron. 证[證] zhèng || chêng \ evidence; proof; testimony. 如 rú || ju \ like; as; as if. 山 shān || shan \ hill; mountain. 白纸黑字, 铁证如山: (Written) in black and white, it is a mass of ironclad evidence; unquestionable and undeniable. (Idiom #117)

§22

One False Step Brought Everlasting Grief

The county magistrate said, "Liquor does not intoxicate, but one intoxicates oneself. A fool 搬起石头打自己的脚,[118] can he blame the stone? 飞蛾扑火,[119] can it blame the flame? A silkworm 作茧自缚,[120] because it 心甘情愿.[121]

---

[118] 搬 bān || pan \ remove; move; take away. 起 qǐ || ch'i \ (used after a verb) upwards; up. 石 shí || shih \ stone; rock. 头[頭] tou || t'ou \ <noun suffix> 石头: stone; rock. 打 dǎ || ta \ strike; beat; hit. 自 zì || tsǔ \ self; one's own. 己 jǐ || chi \ oneself; one's own; personal. 自己: oneself; one's own. 的 de || tê \ <auxiliary word> (used after an attribute) 脚 jiǎo || chiao \ foot; base. 搬起石头打自己的脚: Pick up a rock only to drop it on one's own feet; create problems for oneself. (Idiom #118)

[119] 飞[飛] fēi || fei \ fly. 蛾 é || ê \ moth. 扑[撲] pū || p'u \ throw oneself on. 火 huǒ || huo \ fire. 飞蛾扑火: A moth darts into a flame—bring ruin onto oneself; destroy oneself. (Idiom #119)

[120] 作 zuò || tso \ make; do. 茧[繭] jiǎn || chien \ cocoon. 自 zì || tsǔ \ self; one's own. 缚[縛] fù || fu \ tie up; bind fast. 作茧自缚: Spin a cocoon around oneself; be intangled in one's own trap. (Idiom #120)

[121] 心 xīn || hsin \ heart; intention. 甘 gān || kan \ willingly; pleasant. 情 qíng || ch'ing \ feeling; affection; sentiment. 愿[願] yuàn || yüan \ be willing; hope; wish. 心甘情愿: Willingly; gladly. (Idiom #121)

天网恢恢, 疏而不漏.[122] A thief will be thrown into prison, and he 罪有应得."[123]

Ar Er was sentenced to seven years imprisonment for his breaking in, stealing, lying, beating and shifting blame.

How ever, Ar Er did not 丧尽天良[124]yet, and therefore he cried his heart out. But 生米煮成熟饭,[125]悔之无及.[126]While shedding tears Ah

---

[122] 天 **tiān** || **t'ien** \ sky; heaven. 网[網] **wǎng** || **wang** \ net; network. 恢 **huī** || **hui** \ extensive; vast. 恢恢: extensive; vast. 疏 **shū** || **shu** \ sparse; dispersed; thin. 而 **ér** || **êrh** \ and yet; but; while on the other hand. 不 **bù** || **pu** \ no; not. 漏 **lòu** || **lou** \ leak; be missing; leave out by mistake. 天网恢恢, 疏而不漏: The net of Heaven has large meshes, but it lets nothing through; those who are guilty will not go unpunished—justice has long arms. (Idiom #122)

[123] 罪 **zuì** || **tsui** \ crime; guilt; blame. 有 **yǒu** || **yu** \ have; there is; exist. 应 **yīng** || **ying** \ should; ought to. 得 **dé** || **tê** \ get, obtain, gain. 罪有应得: One deserves one's punishment; a befitting punishment. (Idiom #123)

[124] 丧[喪] **sàng** || **sang** \ lose. 尽[盡] **jìn** || **chin** \ to the limit; exhausted; finished. 天 **tiān** || **t'ien** \ sky; heaven. 良 **liáng** || **liang** \ good; fine. 天良: conscience. 丧尽天良: Have no sense of right and wrong; be without morals. (Idiom #124)

[125] 生 **shēng** || **shêng** \ raw; uncooked. 米 **mǐ** || **mi** \ rice. 煮 **zhǔ** || **chu** \ boil; cook. 成 **chéng** || **ch'êng** \ become; fully developed. 熟 **shú** || **shu** \ cooked; ripe; done.饭[飯] **fàn** || **fan** \ cooked rice; meal. 生米煮成熟饭: The rice is already cooked—it is impossible to undo something. (Idiom #125)

[126] 悔 **huǐ** || **hui** \ regret; repent. 之 **zhī** || **chih** \ <pronoun> (used in place of an objective noun) 无[無] **wú** || **wu** \ not; not have; without. 及 **jí** || **chi** \ reach; come up to; in time for. 无及: too late. 悔之无及: Too late for regrets. (Idiom #126)

Er said to himself, "早知今日，何必当初.[127]I was really 一失足成千古恨！"[128]

Onlookers said, "The guy 偷鸡不着蚀把米,[129]自食其果.[130]He deserved it!"

Ah Er's neighbors said, "Usually 兔子不吃窝边草,[131]but this fellow did exactly the opposite. Fortunately he was caught, otherwise residents

---

[127] 早 **zǎo** || **tsao** \ early; in advance. 知 **zhī** || **chih** \ know; realize; be aware of. 今 **jīn** || **chin** \ today; present-day. 日 **rì** || **jih** \ day; sun; daytime. 今日 today; present; now. 何 **hé** || **hê** \ what; which; how; why. 必 **bì** || **pi** \ must; have to; certainly. 何必: there is no need; why. 当[當] **dāng** || **tang** \ just at (a time or place). 初 **chū** || **ch'u** \ at the beginning of; for the first time; original. 当初: originally; in the first place; at that time. 早知今日，何必当初: If I'd known it would end this way, I would not have done it. (Idiom #127)

[128] 一 **yī** || **i** \ one. 失 **shī** || **shih** \ lose; miss. 足 **zú** || **tsu** \ foot. 失足: lose one's footing; slip; take a wrong step in life. 成 **chéng** || **ch'êng** \ become; fully developed. 千 **qiān** || **ch'ien** \ thousand; a great amount of; a great number of. 古 **gǔ** || **ku** \ ancient; age-old. 千古: through the ages; eternal; for all time. 恨 **hèn** || **hên** \ regret; hate. 一失足成千古恨: One false step can lead to a lifetime's regret. (Idiom #128)

[129] 偷 **tōu** || **t'ou** \ steal. 鸡[雞] **jī** || **chi** \ chicken. 不 **bù** || **pu** \ no; not. 着 **zháo** || **chao** \ <auxilary word> (used as a complement to a verb). 蚀[蝕] **shí** || **shih** \ lose; corrode. 把 **bǎ** || **pa** \ hold; grasp. 米 **mǐ** || **mi** \ rice. 偷鸡不着蚀把米: Try to steal a chicken only to end up losing the rice; seek riches but end up losing everything—go for wool and come home shorn. (Idiom #129)

[130] 自 **zì** || **tsǔ** \ self; one's own. 食 **shí** || **shih** \ eat. 其 **qí** || **ch'i** \ his (her; its; their); he (she, it, they). 果 **guǒ** || **kuo** \ fruit; result; consequence. 自食其果: Eat one's own bitter fruit—deserve the consequence created by one's own actions. (Idiom #130)

[131] 兔 **tù** || **t'u** \ hare; rabbit. 子 **zi** || **tsǔ** (noun suffix). 兔子 hare; rabbit. 不 **bù** || **pu** \ no; not. 吃 **chī** || **ch'ih** \ eat; take. 窝[窩] **wō** || **wo** \ hole; den; nest. 边[邊] **biān** || **pien** \ side. 草 **cǎo** || **ts'ao** \ grass; straw. 兔子不吃窝边草: A hare does not eat the grass near its own hole; a criminal does not destroy his own neighborhood. (Idiom #131)

in the neighborhood would be suspicious and take precautions against each other, and people would be annoyed to 鸡犬不宁."[132]

Because of this, people were full of praises to Xiao Tao, and called him "Our Little Hero." On the other hand, they persuaded Ah Er to start his life afresh.

---

[132] 鸡[雞] jī || chi \ chicken. 犬 quǎn || ch'üan \ dog. 不 bù || pu \ no; not. 宁 [寧] níng || ning \ peaceful; tranquil. 鸡犬不宁: Even chickens and dogs are not left in peace—general unrest; chaos. (Idiom #132)

§23

Killing the Chicken to Frighten the Monkey

Ah Er had a sworn friend, 阿三 (Ah San, ā sān || a san). 近朱者赤, 近墨者黑.[133]Ah San was also a 游手好闲[134]fellow, and often did wrong doings together with Ah Er. The two looked like twin brothers but actually were from different families. They 狼狈为奸,[135]and caused harm in the vicinity.

Ah San thought that Ah Er's failure proved 小不忍则乱大谋.[136] "If I were him, I would have never drunk so much liquor before stealing."

---

[133]   近 jìn || chin \ near; close to; intimate. 朱 zhū || chu \ vermilion; bright red. 者 zhě || chê \ <auxiliary word> (used after an adjective or verb to indicate a group of persons or things) 赤 chì || ch'ih \ red. 墨 mò || mo \ ink; ink stick. 黑 hēi || hei \ black; dark. 近朱者赤, 近墨者黑: He who stays near vermilion gets red, and he who stays near ink gets black—one is influenced by one's peers. (Idiom #133)

[134]   游 yóu || yu \ rove around; swim; tour. 手 shǒu || shou \ hand; personally. 好 hào || hao \ like; love; be fond of. 闲[閒 or 閑] xián || hsien \ not busy; idle; leisure. 游手好闲: Loaf; loiter (usually purposelessly). (Idiom #134)

[135]   狼 láng || lang \ wolf. 狈 bèi || pei \ a legendary wolf. 为 wéi || wei \ do; act; act as; serve as. 奸 jiān || chien \ wicked; evil; treacherous. 狼狈为奸: Act like two wolves in collusion with each other—conspire; connive. (Idiom #135)

[136]   小 xiǎo || hsiao \ small; little; petty; minor. 不 bù || pu \ no; not. 忍 rěn || jên \ forbear; bear; endure. 则[則] zé || tsê \ <conjunction> (used to connect cause, condition, etc. with effect or result) 乱[亂] luàn || luan \ throw into disorder; confuse; mess. 大 dà || ta \ big; large; great. 谋[謀] móu || mou \ stratagem; plan; scheme. 小不忍则乱大谋: A lack of self-control in small things will spoil great plans. (Idiom #136)

Anyhow, the sentence of Ah Er functioned as 杀鸡儆猴[137]to Ah San.

People hoped that both Ah Er and Ah San could keep this bitter lesson in mind, and thoroughly reform themselves.

---

[137] 杀[殺] shā || sha \ kill; slaughter; butcher. 鸡[雞] jī || chi \ chicken. 儆 jǐng || ching \ warn; admonish. 猴 hóu || hou \ monkey. 杀鸡儆猴: Kill the chicken to frighten the monkey—make an example out of somebody; to discipline one in order to show others. (Idiom #137)

§24

Lord Ye Felt as if He Had Invited a Wolf into His House

Hearing of Ah Er's being sentenced, Lord Ye said "good" repeatedly. He then added: "Before I was too bent on dragons, and 玩物丧志,[138]even 引狼入室.[139]Hereafter I definitely will 引以为戒."[140]

---

[138] 玩 **wán** || **wan** \ play; have fun; amuse oneself. 物 **wù** || **wu** \ thing; matter. 丧[喪] **sàng** || **sang** \ lose. 志 **zhì** || **chih** \ will; aspiration; ideal. 玩物丧志: Leisurely pursuits can lead to loss of one's aspiration; too much time spent on one's pastime can sap one's will. (Idiom #138)

[139] 引 **yǐn** || **yin** \ lead; guide; lure; cause; make. 狼 **láng** || **lang** \ wolf. 入 **rù** || **ju** \ enter; go into; join; be admitted into. 室 **shì** || **shih** \ room. 引狼入室: Invite a wolf into the house—let an enemy in; make way for a foe to enter. (Idiom #139)

[140] 引 **yǐn** || **yin** \ make; lead. 以 **yǐ** || **i** \ with; by means of. 为[為] **wéi** || **wei** \ become; be. 戒 **jiè** || **chieh** \ exhort; admonish; warn. 引以为戒: Learn a lesson (from a past mistake); heed a warning. (Idiom #140)

雨过天晴,[141]wild flowers grew 漫山遍野,[142]just like 雨后春笋.[143]Villages felt safer than before and beamed with satisfaction.

Villagers beat drums and gongs, and gave the county magistrate a silk banner embroidered with words of praise "Rid The Peole Of An Evil" to show their gratitude.

The county magistrate declined the villagers' kindness. He said, "I can not 占着茅坑不拉屎.[144]当官不为民作主, 不如回家卖红薯.[145]To

---

141 雨 yǔ || yü \ rain. 过[過] guò || kuo \ pass. 天 tiān || t'ien \ sky. 晴 qíng || ch'ing \ fine; clear. 雨过天晴: The sun shines again after the rain—calm after the rain. (Idiom #141)

142 漫 màn || man \ all over the place; be everywhere. 山 shān || shan \ hill; mountain. 遍 biàn || pien \ all over; everywhere. 野 yě || yeh \ open country; the open. 漫山遍野: All over the mountains and plains; across mountainous and flat country. (Idiom #142)

143 雨 yǔ || yü \ rain. 后[後] hòu || hou \ after; afterwards; later. 春 chūn || ch'un \ spring. 笋[筍] sǔn || sun \ bamboo shoot. 雨后春笋: (Spring up like) bamboo shoots after a spring rain—to mushroom; to flourish. (Idiom #143)

144 占[佔] zhàn || chan \ occupy; hold; take. 着[著] zhe || chê \ <auxiliary word> (indicating an action in progress) 茅 máo || mao \ cogon grass. 坑 kēng || k'êng \ pit; hole; hollow. 茅坑: latrine; outhouse. 不 bù || pu \ no; not. 拉 lā || la \ empty the bowels. 屎 shǐ || shih \ excrement; feces. 拉屎: <informal> empty the bowels; shit. 占着茅坑不拉屎: Sit on the (toilet) seat but not shit; hold on to a post without doing any work and not let anyone else take over; prevent others from using something that one has no use for—be a dog in the manger. (Idiom #144)

145 当[當] dāng || tang \ work as; serve as; be. 官 guān || kuan \ government official; officer. 不 bù || pu \ no; not. 为[為] wèi || wei \ in the interest of; for. 民 mín || min \ the people; civilian. 作 zuò || tso \ do; make; act as. 主 zhǔ || chu \ be in charge of; hold a definite view about something. 作主: decide; take the responsibility for a decision. 如 rú || ju \ be as good as; as if. 不如: not as good as; inferior to. 回 huí || hui \ return; go back. 家 jiā || chia \ home; family; household. 卖[賣] mài || mai \ sell. 红[紅]

73

capture and punish evildoers is our duty, and therefore you do not need to say thanks."

Villagers told Xiao Tao that the county magistrate was an honest and upright official, he had often traveled undercover to investigate complicated cases trying to find the truth.

To the honest official, Xiao Tao 肃然起敬.[146]

---

hóng || hung \ red. 薯 shǔ || shu \ potato; yam. 红薯: yam, sweet potato. 当官不为民作主, 不如回家卖红薯: Being an official but making no good decision for the people, he'd better go back home to sell sweet potatoes; public servants should serve the public well. (Idiom #145)

[146] 肃[肅] sù || su \ respectful; solemn. 然 rán || jan \ (adverb or adjective suffix) 起 qǐ || ch'i \ raise; grow. 敬 jìng || ching \ respect; veneration. 肃然起敬: Be filled with deep veneration; show great respect. (Idiom #146)

§25

Monk Wu Quan Was Ready to Help

Around Xiao Tao, villagers asked this and that. They knew that Xiao Tao was only eleven years old, had lived at western Guan Tian Mountain, had quarreled with his daddy and escaped from home, and then forgot his way home.

Luckily there was a passerby itinerant monk, 悟全 (Wu Quan, **wù quán** || wu ch'üan, which means "realize all") who wanted to go to a place near Guan Tian Mountain. Villagers asked Wu Quan to take Xiao Tao home. Wu Quan, the handsome monk in his mid 30s with 炯炯有神[147]eyes, readily agreed to help.

Villagers invited Xiao Tao and Wu Quan to rest and play several days in their vicinity, but Xiao Tao was eager to go back home. They only rested for one day before starting the return journey.

---

[147] 炯 **jiǒng** || chiung \ bright; shining. 有 **yǒu** || yu \ have; there is; exist. 神 **shén** || shên \ spirit. 炯炯有神: With bright and spirited eyes. (Idiom #147)

§26

Could Cakes in a Drawing Allay Hunger

About one hundred villagers gathered at the entrance of the village to see Xiao Tao and Wu Quan off. They gave Xiao Tao and Wu Quan many gifts such as bamboo shoots, walnuts and dried mushrooms. A little girl was worried about their hunger during the trip, and drew big cakes and gave them to Xiao Tao. "Can 画饼充饥?[148]" Xiao Tao asked. "Of course," answered the little girl. Everyone laughed.

When Wu Quan and Xiao Tao were about to leave, someone pushed a cart and came running over, panting and sweating. This man was no other than Lord Ye. Lord Ye said to Wu Quan that Xiao Tao was too young to walk a long distance, and therefore he had prepared a cart for him.

Wu Quan agreed to take Xiao Tao in the cart to go through the whole journey. However, Xiao Tao declined. He said now that he had been able to come here from home, he should be able to go back home from here. But Wu Quan said; "With the cart we can go faster." Xiao Tao then said, "恭敬不如从命.[149]Many thanks!"

---

[148] 画[畫] huà || hua \ draw; paint; drawing; painting; picture. 饼[餅] bǐng || ping \ a round flat cake. 充 chōng || ch'ung \ fill; stuff; sufficient; full. 饥[饑 or 飢] jī || chi \ be hungry; starved. 画饼充饥: Draw cakes to allay hunger—live on fancy; live off one's fantacy. (Idiom #148)

[149] 恭 gōng || kung \ respectful; reverent. 敬 jìng || ching \ respect; veneration. 不 bù || pu \ no; not. 如 rú || ju \ be as good as; as if. 不如: not as good as; inferior to. 从[從] cóng || ts'ung \ follow; comply with; obey. 命 mìng || ming \ order; command. 恭敬不如从命: It is better to agree respectfully (with one's elders) than to refuse politely. (Idiom #149)

Wu Quan took Xiao Tao in his arms and put him in the cart. Everybody waved farewell. Wu Quan pushed the cart hard. Xiao Tao could not bear to part from the villagers, and he turned his head back and looked at the villagers until they vanished from his sight.

§27

With an Inborn Compass on Head, Xiao Tao Ordered a U-Turn

In a mazelike location Wu Quan got confused and disoriented, he made a 南辕北辙[150]mistake.

Sitting in the cart, facing the front, Xiao Tao felt uneasy. "It is morning, the sun is in the east, and my left hair should be facing the sun if we are going south; but actually my right hair is facing the sun. We must be going in a wrong direction," thought Xiao Tao.

Fortunately, thanks to Xiao Tao's ready-made compass on his head, he found the mistake and told Wu Quan to make a U-turn in time. Otherwise they would never reach their destination.

---

[150] 南 **nán** || nan \ south. 辕[轅] **yuán** || yüan \ shafts of a cart or carriage. 北 **běi** || pei \ north. 辙[轍] **zhé** || chê \ the track of a wheel; rut. 南辕北辙: Try to go south by driving the cart north—create a big setback for one's own objective. (Idiom #150)

§28

A Mantis Tried to Obstruct Xiao Tao's Cart

They had gone less than 10 *li* southward before the cart suddenly stopped. Xiao Tao was almost thrown out of the cart. This was because a big mantis with brawny arms tried to block the way.

"Who has guts to push the cart over my arms?" The mantis shouted to Wu Quan.

Wu Quan and Xiao Tao felt ridiculous. Wu Quan talked to the mantis, "Have you ever heard about the story of 蚍蜉撼树?"[151]

"I have. The ant was very laughable. He 自不量力.[152]But I am different from the ant, because I have strong arms." While saying so, the mantis raised his right arm high to show the well-developed muscles.

---

[151] 蚍 pí || p'i \ a kind of small insects. 蜉 fú || fu \ a kind of very short-lived small insects. 蚍蜉: large ant. 撼 hàn || han \ shake. 树[樹] shù || shu \ tree. 蚍蜉撼树: An ant trying to topple a tree—ludicrously overestimate one's strength and ability. (Idiom #151)

[152] 自 zì || tsŭ\ self; one's own. 不 bù || pu \ no; not. 量 liàng || liang \ measure; estimate; appraise. 力 lì || li \ strength; ability; power. 自不量力: Not know one's own strength; not recognize one's capability; overestimate one's power. (Idiom #152)

Xiao Tao said: "Mantis, actually you and the ant are 半斤八两."[153]Wu Quan said, "Your laughing at the ant was just 五十步笑百步.[154]If you really dare to 螳臂挡车, [155]you will have your body smashed to pieces and your bones grounded to powder—die the most terrible death. You'd better think of the consequence of 以卵击石."[156]

The mantis thought over what Xiao Tao and Wu Quan had warned while his cirri were swaying to the left and to the right, and eventually he straightened his ideas out. "I need to prepare my lunch now," and he climbed towards a cicada on a tree.

The mantis was a careless fellow, and he did not pay attention to an oriole at the back of him. The oriole was hungry too, and thought that the mantis must be delicious! 螳螂捕蝉,黄雀在后.[157]The mantis was happy way too early.

---

[153] 半 **bàn** || pan \ half; semi-. 斤 **jīn** || chin \ a tradition unit of weight (= 0.5 kilogram ~= 1.1 pound). 八 **bā** || pa \ eight. 两[兩] **liǎng** || liang \ a traditional unit of weight (=31.25 grams ~= 1.1 ounces, 16 **liǎng** make 1 **jīn**). 半斤八两: Half a *jin* versus eight *liang*; six of one and half a dozen of the other; same; equal. (Idiom #153)

[154] 五 **wǔ** || wu \ five. 十 **shí** || shih \ ten. 五十: fifty. 步 **bù** || pu \ step; pace. 笑 **xiào** || hsiao \ ridicule; mock; laugh at; laugh; smile. 百 **bǎi** || pai \ hundred. 五十步笑百步: One who retreats fifty paces laughs at one who retreats a hundred—the pot calls the kettle black. (Idiom #154)

[155] 螳 **táng** || t'ang \ mantis. 臂 **bì** || pi \ arm. 挡[擋] **dǎng** || tang \ keep off; ward off; block; get in the way of. 车[車] **chē** || ch'ê \ vehicle. 螳臂挡车: A mantis trying to obstruct a cart—overrate oneself and try to counter a much bigger force. (Idiom #155)

[156] 以 **yǐ** || i \ use; take. 卵 **luǎn** || luan \ egg. 击[擊] **jī** || chi \ beat; hit; strike. 石 **shí** || shih \ stone; rock. 以卵击石: Use an egg to hit a rock—engage in tactics that would bring about one's own destruction against a greater force. (Idiom #156)

[157] 螳 **táng** || t'ang \ mantis. 螂 **láng** || lang \ mantis; roach. 螳螂: mantis. 捕 **bǔ** || pu \ catch; seize; arrest. 蝉 **chán** || ch'an \ cicada. 黄 **huáng** || huang \ yellow; sallow. 雀 **què** || ch'üeh \ finch; sparrow. 黄雀: siskin; oriole. 在 **zài** || tsai \ be; at; exist.后[後] **hòu** || hou \ back; behind; rear. 螳螂捕蝉, 黄雀在后: The mantis stalks the cicada, unaware of the oriole at the back—think only of the profit that lies ahead while forgetting the danger behind. (Idiom #157)

IDIOM #157

§29

Hanging up a Sheep's Head
While Selling Dog Meat

Wu Quan continued to push the cart southward, and before long they came to seashore. The sea looked most magnificent. Wu Quan couldn't help 望洋兴叹,[158]and felt that an individual was merely 沧海一粟[159]among mankind.

They came to a market, and saw an old lady 王 (Wang, **wáng || wang**) was 自卖自夸[160]her melons. Her melons were small, and some of them were already rotten. She praised these melons until 声嘶力竭,[161]but no one patronized her stall.

---

[158] 望 **wàng || wang** \ gaze into the distance. 洋 **yáng || yang** \ ocean; vast. 兴[興] **xīng || hsin** \ start; begin. 叹[嘆] **tàn || t'an** \ sigh; exclaim in admiration. 望洋兴叹: Bemoan one's insignificance before the vast ocean—lament one's incapability when confronted with a grand responsibility. (Idiom #158)

[159] 沧[滄] **cāng || ts'ang** \ (of the sea) deep and blue. 海 **hǎi || hai** \ sea or big lake. 一 **yī || i** \ one. 粟 **sù || su** \ millet. 沧海一粟: A grain of millet in a sea; extremely trivial. (Idiom #159)

[160] 自 **zì || tsǔ**\ self; one's own. 卖[賣] **mài || mai** \ sell; show off. 夸[誇] **kuā || k'ua** \ praise; boast. 自卖自夸: Praise the goods one sells; self-praise; blow one's own trumpet. (Idiom #160)

[161] 声[聲] **shēng || shêng** \ sound; voice. 嘶 **sī || ssǔ**\ hoarse. 力 **lì || li** \ strength; power; ability. 竭 **jié || chieh** \ exhaust; use up. 声嘶力竭 (Also 力竭声嘶): Be hoarse and exhausted; shout until one is almost without voice. (Idiom #161)

Next to Wang was an old man 黄 (Huang, huáng || huang). He was selling the same kind of melons as Wang, however, his melons were big and fresh, 价廉物美.[162]Huang did not praise his melons at all, but people were in a line to buy from him. A young lady said, "I am not familiar with melons, but 不怕不识货, 就怕货比货.[163]Apparently everyone wants to buy from the quiet old man, and let the noisy old woman alone."

Next to the two melon stalls was a mutton restaurant by the name of "The Most Genuine Super Mutton." This restaurant's menu showed many expensive mutton dishes. However, Xiao Tao just wanted to eat a bowl of beef & shrimp noodles to celebrate his twelfth birthday.

Xiao Tao wanted to use the toilet but accidentally entered the kitchen of the restaurant, and only saw dog bodies and tails on the chopping block.

"Are you selling dog meat?" As a pet-lover, Xiao Tao was very angry.

"No, we never have dog meat," the owner said while pointing to a sheep's head in a show window, "You see, we only make delicious mutton dishes."

"You are lying! You 挂羊头, 卖狗肉!"[164]

The restaurant owner gave Xiao Tao a skewer of roasted "mutton cubes," and asked him to "Get out!"

Xiao Tao grabbed the skewer, threw it into a garbage can, and left.

---

[162] 价[價] jià || chia \ price; value. 廉 lián || lien \ low-priced; inexpensive. 物 wù || wu \ thing; matter; content; substance. 美 měi || mei \ beautiful; pretty; very satisfactory; good. 价廉物美. Inexpensive but good, a good bargain; a good buy. (Idiom #162)

[163] 不 bù || pu \ no; not. 怕 pà || p'a \ fear; dread; be afraid of. 识[識] shí || shih \ know; knowledge. 货[貨] huò || huo \ goods; commodity; cargo. 就 jiù || chiu \ just; simply; only. 比 bi || pi \ compare; contrast; match. 不怕不识货, 就怕货比货: Don't worry about not knowing much about the goods; just compare them and you will know which is better. (Idiom #163)

[164] 挂[掛] guà || kua \ hang; put up. 羊 yáng || yang \ sheep. 头[頭] tóu || t'ou \ head. 卖[賣] mài || mai \ sell. 狗 gǒu || kou \ dog. 肉 ròu || jou \ meat; flesh. 挂羊头, 卖狗肉: Hang up a sheep's head to sell dogmeat—misrepresent; pass off something inferior. (Idiom #164)

§30

Set Your Spear against Your Shield

On the other side of the market, a bearish man was selling weapons. He pointed at his spears and said, "My spears are the strongest, and they can penetrate through any shield." Then he pointed at his shields and praised, "These shields are the most excellent, and they can defend you from any spear attack."

Xiao Tao asked a simple question, "以子之矛,攻子之盾,[165]what will happen?"

The bearish man could only scratch his head instead of answering the question about the self-contradictory boast.

---

[165] 以 yǐ || i \ use; take; by means of; with. 子 zǐ || tsŭ\ <formal> you (ancient title of respect for learned or virtuous man). 之 zhī || chih \ <auxiliary word> (used to connect the modifier and the word it modifies) 矛 máo || mao \ spear; lance; pike. 攻 gōng || kung \ attack; take the offensive. 盾 dùn || tun \ shield. 以子之矛, 攻子之盾: Set your spear against your shield—be self-contradictory. (Idiom #165)

§31

Hitting Two Vultures with One Arrow

A crack archer drew his bow widely. He 一箭双雕.[166]

A crowd of onlookers asked him if he had any knack, but he said: "To learn shooting arrows is just like to learn anything else. The only knack

---

[166] 一 yī || i \ one. 箭 jiàn || chien \ arrow. 双[雙] shuāng || shuang \ two; twin; both; dual; <measure> pair. 雕[鵰] diāo || tiao \ vulture; hawk; eagle. 一箭双雕: Hit two vultures with one arrow—kill two birds with one stone. (Idiom #166)

is 勤学苦练,[167]持之以恒.[168]Do not attempt 一步登天.[169]Just like 水滴石穿,[170]persistence is valuable. 只要功夫深, 铁杵磨成针."[171]

By that time, strange sounds came from a thick growth of grass afar. Wow! A tiger was roaring! The crack archer tensed his bow and shot an arrow at once. The arrow did hit the tiger's head, but it fell down to the ground since the target was too far away. The archer's practice proved that 强弩之末[172]could not even break fine silk.

---

[167] 勤 qín || ch'in \ diligent; industrious; hardworking. 学[學] xué || hsüeh \ study; learn. 苦 kǔ || k'u \ painstakingly; doing one's utmost; bitter; hardship. 练[練] liàn || lien \ practice; train; drill. 勤学苦练: Study and train hard. (Idiom #167)

[168] 持 chí || ch'ih \ hold; grasp. 之 zhī || chih \ <pronoun> (used in place of an object) 以 yǐ || i \ with. 恒[恆] héng || hêng \ perseverance; permanent; lasting. 持之以恒: Uphold with perseverance; never give up. (Idiom #168)

[169] 一 yī || i \ one. 步 bù || pu \ step; pace. 登 dēng || têng \ ascend; mount; step on; tread. 天 tiān || t'ien \ sky; heaven. 一步登天: Reach the sky in a single bound—accomplish a great feat in one step; build Rome in one day. (Idiom #169)

[170] 水 shuǐ || shui \ water. 滴 dī || ti \ drip; drop. 石 shí || shih \ stone; rock. 穿 chuān || ch'uan \ pierce through; penetrate; bore through. 水滴石穿: Dripping water wears through a rock—perseverance spells triumph. (Idiom #170)

[171] 只 zhǐ || chih \ only; just; merely. 要 yào || yao \ want; ask for; wish; desire. 只要: so long as; provided. 功 gōng || kung \ skill; work. 夫 fū || fu \ man. 功夫: workmanship; skill; art; work; effort. 深 shēn || shen \ deep; profound. 铁[鐵] tiě || t'ieh \ iron. 杵 chǔ || ch'u \ pestle. 磨 mó || mo \ grind; polish. 成 chéng || ch'êng \ become; turn into. 针 zhēn || chên \ needle. 只要功夫深, 铁杵磨成针: If you work at it hard enough, you can grind an iron rod into a needle—consistent effort will bring about success; little strokes fell great oaks. (Idiom #171)

[172] 强 qiáng || ch'iang \ strong; powerful. 弩 nǔ || nu \ crossbow. 之 zhī || chih \ <auxiliary word> (used between an attribute and the word it modifies) 末 mò || mo \ end; tip. 强弩之末: An arrow at the end of its flight—a depleted or used up force. (Idiom #172)

§32

Riding a Tiger Was Unlike
Riding a Merry-Go-Round

The bearish weapon seller ran all the way towards the tiger, and leapt up with a big stride onto the tiger's back. People clapped in high glee. The tiger was surprised and then ran madly.

Just like a child holding the handles of a wooden horse in kindergarten, the man grabbed the tiger's ears tightly, and did not let the tiger turn his head back to bite him. The tiger ran around here and there for a long time, and made the whole market 人仰马翻.[173]The bearish man 骑虎难下,[174]and uttered moans and groans to himself.

Luckily another tiger threw himself at the tiger with the man on, and provoked the first tiger. The man seized the opportunity, jumped into the air, and fell into a gully, and thus narrowly escaped. He then climbed onto a mountain, 坐山观虎斗.[175]

---

[173] 人 rén || jên \ person, people. 仰 yǎng || yang \ face upward. 马[馬] mǎ || ma \ horse. 翻 fān || fan \ turn upside down or inside out; turn over. 人仰马翻: Men and horses knocked off their feet—be in chaos or confusion. (Idiom #173)

[174] 骑[騎] qí || ch'i \ ride (an animal or bicycle); sit on the back of. 虎 hǔ || hu \ tiger. 难[難] nán || nan \ difficult; hard; troublesome. 下 xià || hsia \ descend; get off; alight. 骑虎难下: He who rides a tiger is afraid to dismount—stuck in the middle of difficult circumstances. (Idiom #174)

[175] 坐 zuò || tso \ sit; take a seat. 山 shān || shan \ hill; mountain. 观[觀] guān || kuan \ look at; watch; observe. 虎 hǔ || hu \ tiger. 斗[鬥] dòu || tou \ fight; struggle against; contend with. 坐山观虎斗: Sit on top of a mountain to

两虎相斗, 必有一伤.[176]The tiger once ridden by the bearish man was full of bloodstains, and the other tiger also got a slight wound.

An old man on crutches came slowly. He murmured, "I really 养虎遗患!"[177]

The story of the new comer was, some twenty years ago he had sincerely thought that 不入虎穴, 焉得虎子?[178]He entered a tiger's lair and got a couple of cubs to rear as pets. When the cubs grew up, 江山易改, 本性难移,[179]they ate one of the man's feet. Today they went out the cage and caused trouble again.

At the critical moment the crack archer shot two arrows with whizzing sounds and hit the noses of the tigers. Both tigers fell down at the report of the arrows.

---

watch the tigers fight—be a bystander and watch others fight (and to gain from it in the end). (Idiom #175)

[176] 两[兩] liǎng || liang \ two. 虎 hǔ || hu \ tiger. 相 xiāng || hsiang \ each other; one another; mutually. 斗[鬥] dòu || tou \ fight; struggle against; contend with. 必 bì || pi \ certainly; must; have to. 有 yǒu || yu \ have; there is; exist. 一 yī || i \ one. 伤[傷] shāng || shang \ wound; injury; hurt. 两虎相斗, 必有一伤: When two tigers fight, one or the other is bound to get hurt. (Idiom #176)

[177] 养[養] yǎng || yang \ raise; rear; keep; grow. 虎 hǔ || hu \ tiger. 遗[遺] yí || i \ leave behind; hand down. 患 huàn || huan \ trouble; peril; disaster. 养虎遗患: Rear a tiger to court disaster—appeasement brings peril. (Idiom #177)

[178] 不 bù || pu \ no; not. 入 rù || ju \ enter; go into. 虎 hǔ || hu \ tiger. 穴 xué || hsüeh \ cave; lair; den; hole. 焉 yān || yen \ how. 得 dé || tê \ get, obtain, gain. 子 zǐ || tsǔ \ son; child. 不入虎穴, 焉得虎子: How can you catch tiger cubs without entering the tiger's lair?—nothing ventured, nothing gained. (Idiom #178)

[179] 江 jiāng || chiang \ river. 山 shān || shan \ mountain; hill. 易 yì || i \ easy. 改 gǎi || kai \ change; transform. 本 běn || pên \ original. 性 xìng || hsing \ nature; character; disposition. 难[難] nán || nan \ difficult; hard; hardly possible. 移 yí || i \ change; alter; move; remove; shift. 江山易改,本性难移: It is easy to change rivers and mountains but hard to change one's nature—hard to teach an old dog new tricks. (Idiom #179)

§33

Scratching an Itch from Outside One's Boot

The bearish man came down from the mountain. The archer said to him, "You look tall and big, but you are actually timid. Why did you get on the back of the tiger, and 虎头蛇尾?"[180]

The bearish man admitted, "I just 哗众取宠."[181] The archer said, "Your self-criticism was only 隔靴搔痒,[182] and therefore you might repeat your

---

[180] 虎 **hǔ** || hu \ tiger. 头[頭] **tóu** || t'ou \ head; beginning; first. 蛇 **shé** || shê \ snake, serpent. 尾 **wěi** || wei \ tail; end. 虎头蛇尾. A tiger's head and a snake's tail; to start a task with great enthusiasm, but to finish without fervor—in like a lion, out like a lamb. (Idiom #180)

[181] 哗[譁] **huá** || hua \ noise; clamor. 众[眾] **zhòng** || chung \ the masses. 取 **qǔ** || ch'ü \ aim at; seek; take; get. 宠[寵] **chǒng** || ch'ung \ dote on; bestow favor on. 哗众取宠: Try to please the public with claptrap; try to impress others with nonsense. (Idiom #181)

[182] 隔 **gé** || kê \ be at a distance from; be apart from; separate; partition. 靴 **xuē** || hsüeh \ boots. 搔 **sāo** || sao \ scratch. 痒 **yǎng** || yang \ itch; tickle. 隔靴搔痒: Scratch an itch from outside one's boot—not get to the root of the problem; fail to strike home. (Idiom #182)

mistake in the future. You should know that this was 性命交关.[183]No one forced you 赶鸭子上架,[184]and you must not 自投罗网!"[185]

---

[183] 性 **xìng** || **hsin** \ nature; character. 命 **mìng** || **ming** \ life. 性命: life (of a human or animal). 交 **jiāo** || **chiao** \ cross; intersect; associate with. 关[關] **guān** || **kuan** \ a key factor; involve; concern. 交关: Have to do with; involve. 性命交关: (A matter) of life and death—critically important. (Idiom #183)

[184] 赶[趕] **gǎn** || **kan** \ drive; drive away. 鸭 **yā** || **ya** \ duck. 子 **zi** || **tsǔ** \ (noun suffix) 上 **shàng** || **shang** \ get on; mount; come or go up; ascend. 架 **jià** || **chia** \ frame; rack; shelf. 赶鸭子上架: Drive a duck onto a perch—force one to do something he is not capable of. (Idiom #184)

[185] 自 **zì** || **tsǔ** \ self; one's own. 投 **tóu** || **t'ou** \ throw oneself into; throw; hurl. 罗[羅] **luó** || **lo** \ a net for catching birds. 网[網] **wǎng** || **wang** \ net; network. 罗网: net; trap. 自投罗网: Throw oneself willingly into the net; jump into the trap; take the bait. (Idiom #185)

§34

A Clumsy Bird Should Start Flying Early

Xiao Tao and Wu Quan watched the farce in the market, and felt that the society itself was a great school in which people could learn many things.

They then went westward. Wu Quan pushed the cart along a path with vigorous strides. They hoped to find a temple to stay in overnight.

The clanks of a bell told them that a temple was nearby. However, they did not know until they entered the temple that this was an empty temple—monks were nowhere to be seen.

Wu Quan said that he had lived in the temple before, and at that time the temple attracted many worshippers. How could it be 面目全非[186]just after half a month?

A pilgrim-like man entered the temple. He said that monks in the temple had heard about the possibility of a dyke break, and they 如坐针毡,[187]and all moved to another uphill temple. 跑得了和尚跑不了庙,[188]and therefore they left over an empty temple here.

---

[186] 面 miàn || mien \ face. 目 mù || mu \ eye. 全 quán || ch'üan \ complete; whole; total; completely. 非 fēi || fei \ not conform to; run counter to. 面目全非: Be changed beyond recognition; unrecognizable. (Idiom #186)

[187] 如 rú || ju \ like; as; as if. 坐 zuò || tso \ sit. 针[針]zhēn || chên \ needle. 毡[氊] zhān || chan \ felt; felt rug; felt blanket. 如坐针毡: Feel as if sitting on a bed of nails; be extremely anxious. (Idiom #187)

[188] 跑 pǎo || p'ao \ run; escape; flee. 得 de || tê \ <auxiliary word> (inserted between a verb and its complement to express possibility or capability). 了 le || lê \ <auxiliary word> (used after a verb to indicate the completion of an action) 和 hé || hê \ gentle; kind; harmonious; peace. 尚 shàng || shang \

"Then why didn't you follow them to go uphill?"

"Over there was already 人满为患,[189]while I seeked quiet. I am preparing for the general examination."

This was a poor scholar. He could not pay for the hotel and had to stay in the temple, which was free.

Xiao Tao was smart, and he asked, "Just now it was you who tolled the bell, right?"

"Yes. Monks allowed me to stay, and their requirement was that I must toll the bell for them. I agreed to be a temporary monk, 做一天和尚撞一天钟."[190]

Wu Quan asked, "The nationwide examination is well in the future. Don't you think it is too early to prepare for it?"

"笨鸟先飞!"[191]Said the scholar, "Someone 平时不烧香, 临时抱佛脚.[192]How can it be enough time?" Both Wu Quan and Xiao Tao nodded assent.

---

esteem; value. 和尚: Buddhist monk. 不 **bù** || **pu** \ no; not. 庙[廟] **miào** || **miao** \ temple. 跑得了和尚跑不了庙: Monks may run away, but the temple can't run with them—those who run away usually leave something behind. (Idiom #188)

[189] 人 **rén** || **jên** \ people; person. 满[滿] **mǎn** || **man** \ full; filled; packed; fill; reach the limit. 为[為] **wéi** || **wei** \ become; be. 患 **huàn** || **huan** \ trouble; peril; disaster. 人满为患: Too many people can lead to disaster—overcrowded with people. (Idiom #189)

[190] 做 **zuò** || **tso** \ be; become. 一 **yī** || **i** \ one. 天 **tiān** || **t'ien** \ day. 和 **hé** || **hê** \ gentle; mild; kind; harmonious; peace. 尚 **shàng** || **shang** \ esteem; value. 和尚: Buddhist monk. 撞 **zhuàng** || **chuang** \ strike. 钟[鐘] **zhōng** || **chung** \ bell; clock. 做一天和尚撞一天钟: Go on tolling the bell as long as one is a monk—get by with minimal effort. (Idiom #190)

[191] 笨 **bèn** || **pên** \ clumsy; stupid; dull; foolish. 鸟[鳥] **niǎo** || **niao** \ bird. 先 **xiān** || **hsien** \ earlier; before; at first; in advance. 飞[飛] **fēi** || **fei** \ fly. 笨鸟先飞: A clumsy bird has to start flying early—the slow one needs to start early to finish a job. (Idiom #191)

[192] 平 **píng** || **p'ing** \ average; common. 时[時] **shí** || **shih** \ time; times; days. 平时: at ordinary times; in normal times. 不 **bù** || **pu** \ no; not. 烧[燒] **shāo** || **shao** \ burn. 香 **xiāng** || **hsiang** \ incense; fragrant; sweet-smelling. 临[臨] **lín** || **lin** \ on the point of; just before; be about to. 临时: at the time when

§35

The Argument among Frogs
about the Shape of Sky

Wu Quan and Xiao Tao stayed at the temple for one night. It was a dog day, and cicadas and frogs chirped all day and night. The next morning they went to the backyard of the temple, and saw three dry wells with different shapes: one was square, one was hexagonal and the last one was round.

In each well a frog was shouting loudly.

"The sky is square!" Shouted the first frog.

"You are wrong. The sky is hexagonal!" Claimed the second.

"Are you all blind? Obviously the sky is round and twice bigger than a bucket!" Quipped the third.

A woodpecker laughed while climbing down from a tree trunk, "井蛙观天[193]is really laughable. They 各持己见,[194]neither was willing to give ground, but actually all were wrong. The sky is spherical and infinite."

---

something is needed or is expected to happen. 抱 **bào** || **pao** \ embrace; clasp; hug. 佛 **fó** || **fo** \ Buddha. 脚[腳 or 脚] **jiǎo** || **chiao** \ foot. 平时不烧香, 临时抱佛脚: Never burn incense when all is well but clasp Buddha's feet in one's time of need—procrastinate until the last minute. (Idiom #192)

[193] 井 **jǐng** || **ching** \ well. 蛙 **wā** || **wa** \ frog. 观[觀] **guān** || **kuan** \ look at; watch; observe. 天 **tiān** || **t'ien** \ sky. 井蛙观天: A frog in a well watches the sky—have a very narrow view. (Idiom #193)

[194] 各 **gè** || **kê** \ each; every. 持 **chí** || **ch' ih** \ hold; grasp. 己 **jǐ** || **chi** \ oneself; one's own. 见 [見] **jiàn** || **chien** \ view; opinion. 各持己见: Each sticks to his own view; each holds his own view stubbornly. (Idiom #194)

Xiao Tao's cricket said to the pecker, "I don't think the earth is elliptical even though I live in a bamboo tube with an egg-shaped section. Their debate was 滑天下之大稽!"[195]

"Let me help them to widen their field of vision," said Xiao Tao while using a bucket to bring frogs up to the ground.

"Oh, the sky is infinite. We were 鼠目寸光[196]before!" All the three frogs gave a loud cry simultaneously.

---

[195] 滑 huá || hua \ slippery; smooth; slip; slide. 天 tiān || t'ien \ sky; heaven. 下 xià || hsia \ below; down; under; underneath. 天下: land under heaven—the world. 之 zhī || chih \ <auxiliary word> (used to connect the modifier and the word it modifies) 大 dà || ta \ big; large; great. 稽 jī || chi \ check; investigate. 滑稽: funny; amusing; comical. 滑天下之大稽: Be the universal laughingstock; be the object of ridicule in the world. (Idiom #195)

[196] 鼠 shǔ || shu \ mouse; rat. 目 mù || mu \ eye. 寸 cùn || ts'un \ a unit of length (= 33.3 mm = 1.312 inch); very little; very short; small. 光 guāng || kuang \ light; ray; brightness; luster. 鼠目寸光: Like a mouse that can see only an inch; can't see beyond one's nose; be very shortsighted. (Idiom #196)

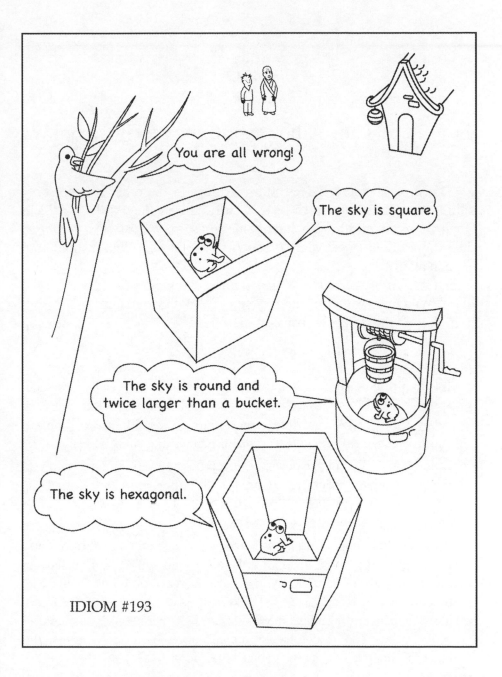

IDIOM #193

95

§36

Not up to Those above, but above Those below

One frog accidentally fell into a well, and the other two not only didn't rescue him, but also 拍手称快,[197]in addition, they 落井下石.[198]Wu Quan shook his head again and again, and said, "阿弥陀佛 (*Amitabha* [i.e. May Buddha preserve us!]) You guys are dog-eat-dog. It should not happen at all!"

The two frogs cursed Wu Quan at once: "You are 狗拿耗子, 多管闲事!"[199]Wu Quan was a little angry. Xiao Tao comforted him, "狗嘴里吐不出象牙.[200]Please do not pay attention to it."

---

[197] 拍 **pāi** || **p'ai** \ clap; pat. 手 **shǒu** || **shou** \ hand. 拍手 clap one's hand; applaud. 称[稱] **chēng** || **ch'êng** \ state; say. 快 **kuài** || **k'uai** \ pleased; happy; gratified. 称快: Express one's gratification. 拍手称快: Clap and cheer (as the enemy or evildoer is being punished). (Idiom #197)

[198] 落 **luò** || **lo** \ fall; drop; go down. 井 **jǐng** || **ching** \ well. 下 **xià** || **hsia** \ (of rain, etc.) fall; drop; descend. 石 **shí** || **shih** \ stone; rock. 落井下石: Drop stones on someone who has fallen into a well—bring a peron down further when he is already down. (Idiom #198)

[199] 狗 **gǒu** || **kou** \ dog. 拿 **ná** || **na** \ seize; capture; hold; take. 耗 **hào** || **hao** \ consume; cost; waste time. 子 **zi** || **tsŭ**\ (noun suffix) 耗子: <dialect> mouse; rat. 多 **duō** || **to** \ many; much; more. 管 **guǎn** || **kuan** \ take care of; be in charge of; manage. 闲[閒] **xián** || **hsien** \ not busy; idle. 事 **shì** || **shih** \ matter; affair; thing; business. 闲事: Other people's business. 狗拿耗子, 多管闲事: A dog trying to catch mice—butt into other peoples business; put one's finger in another's pie. (Idiom #199)

[200] 狗 **gǒu** || **kou** \ dog. 嘴 **zuǐ** || **tsui** \ mouth. 里[裏 or 裡]**li** || **li** \ in; inside. 吐 **tǔ** || **t'u** \ spit. 不 **bù** || **pu** \ no; not. 出 **chū** || **ch'u** \ out. 象 **xiàng** ||

The fallen frog sobbed at the bottom of the well, "I fell down, and you guys 幸灾乐祸.[201] When did I offend you? How can you punish me simply because I disagreed with your opinions about the sky?"

The woodpecker shouted from the tree, "You 祸从口出."[202]

The frog said, "Pecker, I admit that my opinion about the sky was worse than yours, but better than they two anyway. I thought the sky was round. Actually the sky is round, but much bigger than what I thought. They thought the sky was polygonal, and they were much erroneous than me. I was 比上不足, 比下有余."[203]

Wu Quan wanted to rescue the fallen frog, but Xiao Tao said, "Originally he lived in the well. Just let him go back home. There is not much time for us. Let's hurry."

---

hsiang \ elephant. 牙 yá || ya \ tooth. 狗嘴里吐不出象牙: A dog's mouth issues no ivory; a dirty mouth can not say civilized words. (Idiom #200)

201   幸 xìng || hsing \ good fortune; lucky. 灾[災] zāi || tsai \ disaster; misfortune. 乐[樂] lè || lê \ be enjoy; happy. 祸[禍] huò || huo \ misfortunes; disaster. 幸灾乐祸. Take pleasure in other people's bad luck, be happy when others are suffering. (Idiom #201)

202   祸[禍] huò || huo \ misfortune; disaster. 从[從] cóng || ts'ung \ from; through. 口 kǒu || k'ou \ mouth. 出 chū || ch'u \ go or come out. 祸从口出: Disaster comes out of the mouth (i.e. from a loose tongue). (Idiom #202)

203   比 bǐ || pi \ compare; contrast; compete. 上 shàng || shang \ above; upper; up. 不 bù || pu \ no; not. 足 zú || tsu \ sufficient; enough; full. 下 xià || hsia \ below; down; under; underneath. 有 yǒu || yu \ have; there is; exist. 余[餘] yú || yü \ surplus; spare; remaining. 有余: Have a surplus; have enough and to spare. 比上不足, 比下有余: Not up to those above, but above those below—just average; mediocre; merely adequate. (Idiom #203)

§37

The Half-filled Bottle Sloshed,
but the Full Bottle Made No Sound

They entered the temple and wanted to say goodbye to the poor scholar, but they could not find him.

There was a bottle with half-filled water on a table. Wu Quan said that it might be useful when they felt thirsty on their journey. He wrote a note mentioning the bottle (actually a bottle gourd), placed the note on the table, and then took the bottle with him.

On the way, the water in the bottle sloshed a lot. Wu Quan said, "一瓶子不响, 半瓶子晃荡。"[204]Xiao Tao said, "Just drink the water up." He opened the lid of the bottle.

A strange smell assailed Xiao Tao's nose, and made him almost pass out.

---

[204] 一 yī || i \ one; whole. 瓶 píng || p'ing \ bottle; flask. 子 zi || tsŭ\ (noun suffix) 不 bù || pu \ no; not. 响[響] xiǎng || hsiang \ sound; noise; make a sound. 半 bàn || pan \ half; semi-. 晃 huàng || huang \ shake; sway. 荡 [蕩] dàng || tang \ swing; sway; wave. 晃荡: rock; shake; sway. 一瓶子不响, 半瓶子晃荡: The half-filled bottle sloshes, but the full bottle makes no sound—those with little knowledge talks a lot while the truely wise one remain silent. (Idiom #204)

"As a matter of fact this is a bottle of poison," said Wu Quan, "We definitely do not 饮鸩止渴,[205]and let 病从口入."[206]He poured the poison out and threw away the bottle.

They continued their journey hurriedly. Wu Quan already pushed the cart a long way, puffing hard and sweating all over. They wanted to find a grove to relax in the shade, but they only found one tree.

独木不成林.[207]They had to make do with the shade of the only tree, and rested a while in the lonely shade.

Before leaving, Wu Quan used a small knife to cut some twigs, and planted these twigs around the tree.

"What are you doing?" asked Xiao Tao.

"I am transplanting cuttings. Several years later here will be a woody grove. 前人栽树, 后人乘凉.[208]We should do something good for the later generations."

A sculptress and her assistant transported two clay cows to the seaside by means of a horse-drawn carriage, and then pushed the cows into the sea. Xiao Tao and Wu Quan felt it was very strange.

---

[205] 饮[飲] yǐn || yin \ drink. 鸩[酖] zhèn || chên \ poisoned wine. 止 zhǐ || chih \ stop. 渴 kě || k'ê \ thirsty. 饮鸩止渴: Drink poison to quench thirst—take irrational measures. (Idiom #205)

[206] 病 bìng || ping \ illness; sickness; disease. 从[從] cóng || ts'ung \ from; through. 口 kǒu || k'ou \ mouth. 入 rù || ju \ enter; go in to. 病从口入: Sickness goes in by the mouth; Disease comes from food. (Idiom #206) (Always followed by 祸从口出, see Idiom #202)

[207] 独[獨] dú || tu \ only; single; solely; alone. 木 mù || mu \ tree; wood. 不 bù || pu \ no; not. 成 cheng || ch'êng \ become; turn into. 林 lin || lin \ forest; woods; grove. 独木不成林: One tree does not make a forest—a single person can not make a big difference. (Idiom #207)

[208] 前 qián || ch'ien \ front; ahead; before; preceding; former. 人 rén || jên \ person; people. 前人: forefathers; predecessors. 栽 zāi || tsai \ plant; grow. 树[樹] shù || shu \ tree. 后[後] hòu || hou \ back; behind; after; later. 后人: Later generations; descendants. 乘 chéng || ch'êng \ take advantage of. 凉[涼 or 凉] liáng || liang \ cool; cold. 乘凉: relax in a cool place. 前人栽树, 后人乘凉: One generation planted the trees, in whose shade another generation rests—benefit from the previous generation's hardwork; laboring to make a better future for later generations. (Idiom #208)

99

The sculptress said, "You are proving 少见多怪.[209]It is too hot, and we just let our cows take a cold bath."

泥牛入海,[210]they never returned. The sculptress and her assistant could only go back with the empty carriage.

[209] 少 shǎo || shao \ few; little; less; lack. 见[見] jiàn || chien \ see; catch sight of. 多 duō || to \ many; much; more. 怪 guài || kuai \ strange; odd. 少见多怪: The less one has seen, the more one has to wonder at; those who are not knowledgeable marvel at many things. (Idiom #209)

[210] 泥 ní || ni \ mud. 牛 niú || niu \ ox; cattle; cow. 入 rù || ju \ enter; go into. 海 hǎi || hai \ sea or big lake. 泥牛入海: Clay cows entered the sea—lost forever. (Idiom #210)

§38

A Foot Might Prove Short
while an Inch Might Prove Long

The curtain of night fell while the moon rose. Reflecting in the water, the moon looked very nice.

Several young girls were enjoying the beautiful full moon. One of them said, "What does 嫦娥 (Chang E, cháng é || ch'ang e \ the lady in the moon; the Chinese moon goddess) look like? I can not see her clearly. We just fish the moon out of the water and have a detailed look!"

The other girls felt this was a good idea, and scooped up some water with their hands, 水中捞月.[211]

Xiao Tao laughed. How could the girls be so "clever?" He said, "The longer the hair, the shorter the wisdom. The saying is correct!" But Wu Quan said that such thought regarding men as superior to women was not right and no good.

Xiao Tao made a joke: "Your hair is shorter than mine, and you should be cleverer than me!"

Wu Quan said, "Cleverness has nothing to do with the length of hair. In addition, 尺有所短, 寸有所长.[212]No one is perfect."

---

[211] 水 shuǐ || shui \ water; a general term for rivers, lakes, seas, etc. 中 zhōng || chung \ in; middle among; amidst. 捞[撈] lāo || lao \ fish for; scoop up from the water. 月 yuè || yüeh \ the moon. 水中捞月: Fish the reflection of the moon in water—to work in vain; futile efforts. (Idiom #211)

[212] 尺 chǐ || ch'ih \ a unit of length (= 0.333 meter = 1.093 foot = 10 寸). 有 yǒu || yu \ have; there is; exist. 所 suǒ || so \ <auxiliary word> (used after a verb to form a possessive case) its. 短 duǎn || tuan \ short; weak point;

Xiao Tao felt a little sleepy and Wu Quan let him lie down and rest a while under a big tree.

Unexpectedly a leaf fell down from the tree, and upon Xiao Tao's head. Xiao Tao thought that fall season already quietly came, 一叶知秋.[213]

The leaf fell exactly on his eyes and blocked his vision.

Another strange thing was: two soybeans that had dropped on the top of the kitchen range when cooking beans at the old fisherman's home (see section 5) jumped into his ears.

Xiao Tao could neither see nor hear, and became both blind and deaf. He was frightened and screamed until he became hoarse and exhausted.

He took off the leaf and his eyes could see again. He turned his head to the left and the bean in his left ear dropped out; and then he did the same to the right and let another bean get out. His sense of listening recovered.

Eventually he was woken up by Wu Quan, and found that it was a dream again.

"I will never 一叶障目，两豆塞耳[214]again," Xiao Tao murmured.

---

fault. 寸 **cùn** || **ts'un** \ a unit of length (= 0.333 decimeter = 1.312 inch = 0.1尺). 长[長] **cháng** || **ch'ang** \ long; strong point; forte. 尺有所短，寸有所长: Sometimes a foot may prove short while an inch may prove long—everyone has strengths and weaknesses. (Idiom #212)

[213]　一 **yī** || **i** \ one; single. 叶[葉] **yè** || **yeh** \ leaf; foliage. 知 **zhī** || **chih** \ inform; know; realize; be aware of. 秋 **qiū** || **ch'iu** \ autumn; fall. 一叶知秋: The falling of one leaf heralds the autumn—straws in the wind; a small hint of a coming development. (Idiom #213)

[214]　一 **yī** || **i** \ one; single. 叶[葉] **yè** ||**yeh** \ leaf; foliage. 障 **zhàng** || **chang** \ obstruct; block. 目 **mù** || **mu** \ eye. 两[兩] **liǎng** || **liang** \ two. 豆 **dòu** || **tou** \ legumes; beans; peas. 塞 **sāi** || **sai** \ fill in; squeeze in; stuff. 耳 **ěr** || **êrh** \ ear. 一叶障目，两豆塞耳: Shut one's view by a leaf before the eyes and shut one's hearing by two beans in the ears—have one's senses of the important overshadowed by the unimportant. (Idiom #214)

§39

"While the Water Can Bear the Boat, It Can also Sink the Boat"

A sailboat was berthing at the wharf, which was located at the endpoint of a river. Xiao Tao said, "If we go by boat we will arrive early. The favorable wind will save labor and time." Without thinking Wu Quan agreed. An old boatman let them board his boat.

Waves lapped against the sides of the boat. In the wake of their leaving the berth, the direction of wind changed. The boatman lowered the sails at once, and rowed his sweep hard. But the boat could not move forward, and it actually moved backward.

The old boatman said to Xiao Tao and Wu Quan, "逆水行舟, 不进则退.[215] You'd better help to row the oars, please!"

Wu Quan strained hard at the oars immediately, but Xiao Tao was rather unwilling to do anything. The old boatman knew that the little boy

---

[215] 逆 nì || ni \ go against; contrary; counter; converse; inverse. 水 shuǐ || shui \ water; general term for rivers or lakes, seas. etc. 行 xíng || hsing \ go; travel. 舟 zhōu || chou \ boat. 不 bù || pu \ no; not. 进[進] jìn || chin \ advance; move forward. 则[則] zé || tsê \ <conjunction> (used to indicate condition) 退 tuì || t'ui \ move back; retreat. 逆水行舟, 不进则退: When sailing against the current, either you keep forging ahead or you will be pushed falling behind—one must persevere in order to forge ahead. (Usually this idiom is for describing "one's studies.")(Idiom #215)

did not understand the importance of 同舟共济,[216]and gave up asking for help. Xiao Tao said, "Just now we had a favorable wind, how come it suddenly changed?"

"No one knows but Buddha above," answered the old boatman. However, Xiao Tao disagreed with him and asked: "Why don't you say 'No one knows but God above'?" Apparently Xiao Tao believed in God rather than Buddha.

"Grandpa [used by children in addressing an old man], do you have any tea?" The old man gave a cup of water to Xiao Tao.

Xiao Tao was going to drink, but suddenly big waves made the boat tossing about and the water in the cup was all gone. 覆水难收.[217] "Sorry, I have only that little water. You can only wait till we dock the boat."

A surge made the boat sway severely. Wu Quan asked Xiao Tao to join the oarsmen. "水能载舟,亦能覆舟.[218]Only if we 齐心协力[219]we can overcome the difficulty."

Xiao Tao then exerted all his strength to row the boat, even though it was 勉为其难[220]for him.

---

[216] 同 tóng || t'ung \ together; in common. 舟 zhōu || chou \ boat. 共 gòng || kung \ common; general; together. 济[濟] jì || chi \ aid; help; benefit. 同舟共济: People in the same boat help each other—people in the same difficult situation help each other. (Idiom #216)

[217] 覆 fù || fu \ <formal> overturn; upset. 水 shuǐ || shui \ water. 难[難] nán || nan \ difficult; hard. 收 shōu || shou \ collect; gather in; take in. 覆水难收: Spilled water can not be gathered up—what is done can hardly be undone. (Idiom #217)

[218] 水 shuǐ || shui \ water. 能 néng || nêng \ can; be able to; be capable of. 载 [載] zài || tsai \ carry; hold; be loaded with. 舟 zhōu || chou \ boat. 亦 yì || i \ also; too. 覆 fù || fu \ overturn; upset. 水能载舟,亦能覆舟: While water can bear the boat, it can also sink the boat. (Idiom #218) (Usually "water" is a metaphor for "people," while "boat" is a metaphor for "ruler".)

[219] 齐[齊] qí || ch'i \ together; simultaneously. 心 xīn || hsin \ heart; feeling; intention. 协[協] xié || hsieh \ joint; common. 力 lì || li \ force; strength; ability. 齐心协力: Work as one; work together. (Idiom #219)

[220] 勉 miǎn || mien \ exert oneself to do; strive. 为[為] wéi || wei \ do; act. 其 qí || ch'i \ his (her; its; their). 难[難] nán || nan \ difficulty; difficult; hard; troublesome. 勉为其难: Undertake to do what one knows is beyond one's ability or power—to endure pain with courage. (Idiom #220)

§40

More Haste, Less Speed

When the boat was approaching a bridge, Xiao Tao was afraid, for the bridge opening was not very wide. The boatman told him, "车到山前必有路, 船到桥头自会直."[221]It easily passed through.

The direction of the wind changed again, and the boatman hurriedly hoisted the sails. The boat 乘风破浪,[222]and soon reached the destination.

However, in comparison with walking, traveling by boat was slower. Xiao Tao had hoped 事半功倍[223]but ended in 事倍功半.[224]Wu Quan said,

---

[221] 车[車] chē || ch'ê \ vehicle. 到 dào || tao \ arrive; reach. 山 shān || shan \ hill; mountain. 前 qián || ch'ien \ front; forward; ahead. 必 bì || pi \ certainly; surely; must; have to. 有 yǒu || yu \ have; there is; exist. 路 lù || lu \ road; path; way. 船 chuán || ch'uan \ boat; ship. 桥[橋] qiáo || ch'iao \ bridge. 头[頭] tóu || t'ou \ end. 桥头: either end of a bridge. 自 zì || tsǔ \ certainly 会[會] huì || hui \ can; be able to. 直 zhí || chih \ straight; straighten. 车到山前必有路, 船到桥头自会直: The cart will find its way round the hill when it gets there, and the boat will straighten to pass the bridge opening when it approaches—things will work themselves out. (Idiom #221)

[222] 乘 chéng || ch'êng \ ride; take advantage of. 风[風] fēng || fêng \ wind. 破 pò || p'o \ cleave; break; cut. 浪 làng || lang \ wave. 乘风破浪: Ride the wind and cleave the waves; go with the wind and the waves. (Idiom #222)

[223] 事 shì || shih \ thing; work. 半 bàn || pan \ half; semi-. 功 gōng || kung \ result; achievement; merit. 倍 bèi || pei \ double; twice as much; times;—fold. 事半功倍: Make half the effort to get twice the result. (Idiom #223)

[224] See note # 223. 事倍功半: Make twice the effort to get half the result. (Idiom #224)

"I did not consider the idea thoroughly. I simply wanted to sit in a boat with favorable wind, and that resulted in 欲速则不达."[225]

---

[225] 欲 yù || yü \ wish; want; desire. 速 sù || su \ fast; rapid; quick; speedy. 则[則] zé || tsê \ <conjunction> (used to indicate contrast) 不 bù || pu \ no; not. 达 [達] dá || ta \ reach; attain. 欲速则不达: Haste brings no success; the more one hurries, the less one accomplishes—haste makes waste. (Idiom #225)

§41

He Who Helped Others Helped Himself

They gave the boatman silver, but he declined. "I wanted to sail here, and just brought you incidentally. You helped to row the boat, and I should say thank you!"

Wu Quan and Xiao Tao said that this was the silver he should accept, but the old boatman firmly declined. He said, "助人为乐[226]is my creed. I do not believe '有钱能使鬼推磨.'[227] 与人方便, 自己方便!"[228]

Wu Quan said, "You are really a well-doer. 善有善报, 恶有恶报.[229]*Amitabha* Buddha!" He put his palms together before the old boatman, and bowed his thankfulness to him. Xiao Tao also expressed his thankfulness and said goodbye to the boatman.

---

[226] 助 zhù || chu \ help; assist; aid. 人 rén || jên \ person; people. 为[為] wéi || wei \ do; act; become. 乐[樂] lè || lê \ happy; joyful. 助人为乐: Feel happy to help others; fulfill oneself through helping the others. (Idiom #226)

[227] 有 yǒu || yu \ have; there is. 钱[錢] qián || ch'ien \ money. 能 néng || nêng \ can; be able to. 使 shǐ || shih \ make; cause; enable. 鬼 guǐ || kuei \ ghost; spirit. 推 tuī || t'ui \ push. 磨 mò || mo \ millstones. 有钱能使鬼推磨: With money you can make the devil turn the millstone—money talks. (Idiom #227)

[228] 与[與] yǔ || yü \ give; offer; grant. 人 rén || jên \ person; people. 方 fāng || fang \ method. 便 biàn || pien \ convenient. 方便: Convenient. 自 zì || tsǔ \ self; one's own. 己 jǐ || chi \ oneself; one's own; personal. 自己: Oneself; own. 与人方便, 自己方便: The one who helps others helps himself. (Idiom #228)

[229] 善 shàn || shan \ good; virtuous; friendly. 有 yǒu || yu \ have; there is; exist. 报[報] bào || pao \ retribution. 恶[惡] è || ê \ evil; vice; wickedness. 善有善报, 恶有恶报: Good is rewarded with good, and evil with evil—the consequences of one's actions will eventually come back to benefit or harm one. (Idiom #229)

§42

To Xiao Tao's Great Surprise

Thinking of his parents with affection, Wu Quan 捷足先登[230]jumped to the bank after the boat had docked. Then Xiao Tao also got on the bank, and they went to see Wu Quan's parents.

To Xiao Tao's great surprise, Wu Quan's parents were just the old fisherman and wife he had met before. The old couple saw that their son was back home with the little kid Xiao Tao, and felt very happy. But Xiao Tao felt embarrassed since he had spoken impolitely to them, and had left without saying goodbye.

The old fisherman did feel Xiao Tao's embarrassment, and said frankly, "人非圣贤, 孰能无过?[231]Moreover, you are a little boy. Just forget about it!"

---

[230] 捷 jié || chieh \ swift; nimble; quick. 足 zú || tsu \ foot. 先 xiān || hsien \ earlier; before; first; in advance. 登 dēng || têng \ ascend; mount. 捷足先登: The swift-footed arrive first—the early bird gets the worm. (Idiomn #230)

[231] 人 rén || jên \ person; people. 非 fēi || fei \ be not. 圣[聖] shèng || shêng \ saint; sage. 贤[賢] xián || hsien \ person of virtue (or merit); person of outstanding worth. 孰 shú || shu \ how; who; which; what. 能 néng || nêng \ can; be able to; be capable of. 无[無] wú || wu \ not have; there is not; without. 过[過] guò || kuo \ fault; mistake. 人非圣贤, 孰能无过: Men are not saints, how can they be free from faults; no one is without faults. (Idiom #231)

人逢喜事精神爽，月到中秋分外明.[232]That day was Mid-autumn Festival, and everyone enjoyed 月饼 (yuè bǐng || yüeh ping, moon cakes). The old fisherman's family was reunited. They looked back at happy events, and nothing could be more content.

[232] 人 rén || jên \ person; people. 逢 féng || fêng \ meet; come upon. 喜 xǐ || hsi \ happy; delighted; pleased. 事 shì || shih \ matter; affair; thing. 喜事: happy event; wedding. 精 jīng || ching \ energy; spirit. 神 shén || shên \ spirit; mind; god. 精神: spirit; mind. 爽 shuǎng || shuang \ bright; clear; feel well. 月 yuè || yüeh \ the moon. 到 dào || tao \ arrive; reach. 中 zhōng || chung \ mid; center; middle. 秋 qiū || ch'iu \ autumn; fall. 中秋: The Mid-autumn Festival (15th day of the 8th lunar month). 分 fēn || fên \ point; mark. 外 wài || wai \ beyond; outer; outward; outside. 分外: particularly; especially. 明 míng || ming \ bright; brilliant; light. 人逢喜事精神爽，月到中秋分外明: People in a happy event are spirited, and the moon on Mid-autumn Festival is particularly bright. (Idiom #232)

§43

Calling a Deer a Horse

Wu Quan told Xiao Tao, "When I was at your age I dreamt to be a strategist, and often 纸上谈兵[233]with other kids. Later, I saw too many bad things such as 口是心非,[234]阳奉阴违,[235]尔虞我诈,[236]指鹿为马,[237]and

---

[233] 纸[紙] zhǐ || chih \ paper. 上 shang || shang \ (used after a noun) on. 谈[談] tán || t'an \ talk; chat; discuss. 兵 bīng || ping \ soldier; army; troops; military. 纸上谈兵: Fight only on paper; philosophize without taking any real action. (Idiom #233)

[234] 口 kǒu || k'ou \ mouth. 是 shì || shih \ yes; right; correct. 心 xīn || hsin \ heart; mind; intention. 非 fēi || fei \ no; wrong; incorrect; run counter to; not. 口是心非: Say yes but mean no; say one thing but mean another. (Idiom #234)

[235] 阳[陽] yáng || yang \ open; overt; the face side. 奉 fèng || fêng \ give or present with respect; esteem; revere. 阴[陰] yīn || yin \ hidden; secret; the back side. 违[違] wéi || wei \ disobey; violate. 阳奉阴违: Overtly agree and covertly oppose; comply in public and oppose in private; be hypocritical. (Idiom #235)

[236] 尔[爾] ěr || êrh \ <formal> thou; you. 虞 yú || yü \ <formal> deceive; cheat; fool. 我 wǒ || wo \ I; we; self. 诈[詐] zhà || cha \ swindle; pretend; bluff somebody into giving something. 尔虞我诈: Cheat one another. (Idiom #236)

[237] 指 zhǐ || chih \ indicate; point at. 鹿 lù || lu \ deer. 为[為] wéi || wei \ be. 马[馬] mǎ || ma \ horse. 指鹿为马: Point at a deer and call it a horse—purposefully lie. (Idiom #237)

in quite a few places 只许州官放火, 不许百姓点灯. [238]上梁不正下梁歪,[239]and that was why corrupt officials were 多如牛毛,[240]but honest official were 寥若晨星."[241]

---

[238] 只 zhǐ || chih \ only; merely. 许[許] xǔ || hsü \ allow; permit. 州 zhōu || chou \ an administrative division under the province. 官 guān || kuan \ government official. 放 fàng || fang \ set off. 火 huǒ || huo \ fire. 放火: commit arson; set on fire. 不 bù || pu \ no; not. 百 bǎi || pai \ hundred. 姓 xìng || hsin \ surname; family name. 百姓: ordinary people. 点[點] diǎn || tien \ light; kindle; burn. 灯[燈] dēng || têng \ lamp; lantern. 点灯: to light lamps or lanterns. 只许州官放火, 不许百姓点灯: The magistrates are free to burn down houses, while the ordinary people are forbidden even to light lamps (usually describe oppressive and corrupt public officials). (Idiom #238)

[239] 上 shàng || shang \ upper; up; higher. 梁 liáng || liang \ roof beam. 不 bù || pu \ no; not. 正 zhèng || chêng \ straight; upright. 下 xià || hsia \ below; down; lower; inferior. 歪 wāi || wai \ askew; aslant; crooked. 上梁不正下梁歪: If the upper beam is not straight, the lower ones will go aslant—when one's superior or predecessor is corrupt or unworthy, one will follow in his footsteps. (Idiom #239)

[240] 多 duō || to \ many; much; more. 如 rú || ju \ like; as; can compare with. 牛 niú || niu \ ox; cow. 毛 máo || mao \ hair. 多如牛毛: As many as the hairs on a cow; countless; innumerable. (Idiom #240)

[241] 寥 liáo || liao \ few; scanty. 若 ruò || jo \ like; as; as if; seem. 晨 chén || ch'ên \ morning. 星 xīng || hsing \ star. 晨星: morning stars. 寥若晨星: As rare as the morning stars; very few. (Idiom #241)

111

§44

Wu Quan Was as Silent as a Cicada in Cold Weather

Wu Quan continued to talk, although little Xiao Tao could only understand very little. "A lot of people lived in 水深火热[242]without any help. They lived度日如年,[243]and they could do nothing except 指桑骂槐.[244]For the corruption in officialdom, I 深恶痛绝,[245]but I 心有余而力

---

[242] 水 shuǐ || shui \ water. 深 shēn || shên \ deep. 火 huǒ || huo \ fire. 热[熱] rè || jê \ heat; hot. 水深火热: Deep water and scorching fire—bitterly suffering; deprivation. (Idiom #242)

[243] 度 dù || tu \ spend; pass. 日 rì || jih \ day; daily. 如 rú || ju \ like; as; as if. 年 nián || nien \ year. 度日如年: One day seems like a year—subsist in hardship. (Idiom #243)

[244] 指 zhǐ || chih \ point at; indicate; finger. 桑 sāng || sang \ mulberry. 骂[罵] mà || ma \ (verbally) abuse; curse; scold. 槐 huái || huai \ Chinese scholartree; locust; a type of tree. 指桑骂槐: Point at the mulberry and abuse the locust—point at one but curse another; make indirect accusations. (Idiom #244)

[245] 深 shēn || shên \ deep; deeply. 恶[惡] wù || wu \ loathe; dislike; hate. 痛 tòng || t'ung \ bitterly; extremely. 绝[絕] jué || chüeh \ cut off; sever. 深恶痛绝: Hate bitterly; loathe. (Idiom #245)

不足²⁴⁶and 孤掌难鸣,²⁴⁷I could not do anything about it. Eventually I was forced to 噤若寒蝉,²⁴⁸and renounced my family to become a monk."

---

246 心 xīn || hsin \ heart; mind; feeling; intention. 有 yǒu || yu \ have; there is; exist. 余[餘] yú || yü \ extra; surplus; spare; remaining. 有余: have a surplus; have enough and to spare. 而 ér || êrh \ and yet; but; while on the other hand. 力 lì || li \ ability; power; strength. 不 bù || pu \ no; not. 足 zú || tsu \ sufficient; enough; ample; full. 心有余而力不足: One's capability falls short of one's wishes; the heart is willing, but the flesh is weak. (Idiom #246)

247 孤 gū || ku \ alone; solitary; isolated. 掌 zhǎng || chang \ palm. 难[難] nán || nan \ difficult; hard; hardly possible. 鸣[鳴] míng || ming \ make a sound. 孤掌难鸣: To clap with one hand is impossible—it is hard to accomplish something without any help from others. (Idiom #247)

248 噤 jìn || chin \ keep silent; shiver. 若 ruò || jo \ like; seem; as if. 寒 hán || han \ cold. 蝉[蟬] chán || ch'an \ cicada. 噤若寒蝉: As silent as a cicada in cold weather—stay silent with fear. (Idiom #248)

§45

"The Spectator Sees the Chess Game Better Than the Players"

往事如烟.[249]After listening to his son's words, the old fisherman sighed with emotion. He said to Wu Quan, "Do you feel 英雄无用武之地?"[250]

"No. I am not a hero at all."

---

[249] 往 **wǎng** || wang \ past; previous. 事 **shì** || shih \ affair; event; matter; thing. 如 **rú** || ju \ like; as; as if. 烟[煙] **yān** || yen \ smoke; mist; vapor. 往事如烟: Past events have vanished like smoke—forgotten events in one's past. (Idiom #249)

[250] 英 **yīng** || ying \ outstanding person. 雄 **xióng** || hsiung \ male; powerful; mighty. 英雄: hero; heroine. 无[無] **wú** || wu \ have not; there is not; without. 用 **yòng** || yung \ use; employ; apply. 武 **wǔ** || wu \ skill; force. 用武: use force; display one's abilities or talents. 之 **zhī** || chih \ <auxiliary word> (used to connect the modifier and the word it modifies) 地 **dì** || ti \ place; fields; ground. 英雄无用武之地: A hero with no place to display his superior ability—have no means to put one's skills and abilities into practice. (Idiom #250)

"Your shortcoming is 孤芳自赏,[251]but 亡羊补牢, 犹未为晚.[252]You can 改弦易辙,[253]resume secular life, and accomplish something."

"No, dad," Wu Quan spoke in a halting way, "In this world 当局者迷, 旁观者清.[254]I have already seen through the vanity of the world, and I only want to be a monk. It is impossible for me to 匡世济民,[255]but I can persuade people to do good deeds. And this is the meaning of my life."

---

[251] 孤 gū || ku \ solitary; isolated; alone. 芳 fāng || fang \ sweet-smelling; fragrant. 自 zì || tsŭ \ self; one's own. 赏 shǎng || shang \ admire; enjoy; appreciate. 孤芳自赏: A lonesome flower in love with its own fragrance; a lonely person admiring his own purity. (Idiom #251)

[252] 亡 wáng || wang \ flee; run away; lose; die; deceased. 羊 yáng || yang \ sheep. 补[補] bǔ || pu \ mend; patch; repair. 牢 láo || lao \ pen; fold. 犹 [猶] yóu || yu \ still. 未 wèi || wei \ have not; did not; not. 为[為] wéi || wei \ be; become; mean. 晚 wǎn || wan \ late. 亡羊补牢, 犹未为晚: It is not too late to mend the fold even after some sheep have run away—there is still time for remediation. (Idiom #252)

[253] 改 gǎi || kai \ change; correct. 弦 xián || hsien \ string. 易 yì || i \ change; exchange. 辙[轍] zhé || chê \ the direction of traffic; the track of a wheel; rut. 改弦易辙: Change one's course; strike out on a new way. (Idiom #253)

[254] 当[當] dāng || tang \ direct; manage; be in charge of. 局 jù || chü \ game; situation. 者 zhě || chê \ <auxiliary word> (used after an adjective or a verb or a phrase as a substitute for a person or a group of persons.) one who; those who. 迷 mí || mi \ be confused; be perplexed. 旁 páng || p'ang \ side. 观[觀] guān || kuan \ look at; watch; observe. 清 qīng || ch'ing \ clear; unmixed; clarified. 当局者迷, 旁观者清: The spectator sees the chess game better than the players—a third party who is not enmeshed in a particular situation has the most unbiased view. (Idiom #254)

[255] 匡 kuāng || k'uang \ assist; save. 世 shì || shih \ world. 济[濟] jì || chi \ benefit; aid; relieve; help. 民 mín || min \ the people. 匡世济民: Save the world and benefit the people. (Idiom #255)

§46

The Taste Was Just Like Chewing Wax

"Well," said Wu Quan's father, "Many people risked their lives in search of money and fame, yet once they had them, they felt 味同嚼蜡.[256] I won't interfere in your choice."

Wu Quan thanked his father for not interfering, and added, "It is late now. Let us sleep. Tomorrow I will go."

"Where will you go?" Everyone asked.

"Monks drift all around the country, 四海为家,"[257] replied Wu Quan.

---

[256] 味 wèi || wei \ taste; flavor. 同 tóng || t'ung \ same; similar; be the same as. 嚼 jiáo || chiao \ chew. 蜡[蠟] là || la \ wax. 味同嚼蜡: The taste is like chewing wax—bored; dull; unexciting. (Idiom #256)

[257] 四 sì || ssŭ \ four. 海 hǎi || hai \ sea. 四海: The four seas; the whole country; the whole world. 为[為] wéi || wei \ become; be. 家 jiā || chia \ home. 四海为家: Make one's home wherever one is; everywhere can be home. (Idiom #257)

§47

The Difference between With and Without Justice

That night, Xiao Tao and Wu Quan slept together, and 依依不舍.[258] Xiao Tao said. "Wu Quan, you helped me a lot, and taught me many things. You are my teacher. I do not know how to thank you!"

Wu Quan said, "Please don't say so. 三人行, 必有我师.[259] You also have many respects I should learn from."

The next morning, the old fisherman and his wife got up very early, and prepared rich breakfast for Wu Quan and Xiao Tao, but Wu Quan only ate vegetarian food.

The old woman looked at her son 泪如泉涌.[260] Wu Quan persuaded his mother: "人生如梦.[261] It is better to wake up from the dream laughing than crying."

---

[258] 依 yī || i \ depend on. 不 bù || pu \ no; not. 舍[捨] shě || shê \ give up; abandon. 依依不舍: Can not bear parting. (Idiom #258)

[259] 三 sān || san \ three. 人 rén || jên \ person; people. 行 xíng || hsin \ go; walk; travel. 必 bì || pi \ certainly; surely. 有 yǒu || yu \ have; there is; exist. 我 wǒ || wo \ I. 师 shī || shih \ teacher. 三人行, 必有我师: Where there are three people walking together, one of them must be able to teach me something. (Idiom #259)

[260] 泪[淚] lèi || lei \ tear. 如 rú || ju \ like; as; as if; can compare with. 泉 quán || ch'üan \ spring. 涌 yǒng || yung \ gush; well; spring; surge. 泪如泉涌: Tears welling up in one's eyes; tears overflow one's eyes. (Idiom #260)

[261] 人 rén || jên \ person; people. 生 shēng || shêng \ life. 人生: life. 如 rú || ju \ like; as; as if; can compare with. 梦[夢] mèng || mêng \ dream. 人生如梦: Life is but a dream; life is too short. (Idiom #261)

The old fisherman said to his son, "Although you are not a fisherman, I still want you to remember two sayings related to fishing. First, do not 三天打鱼, 两天晒网.[262]Second, 任凭风浪起, 稳坐钓鱼船."[263]

Xiao Tao said goodbye to the old fisherman and his wife. Wu Quan bade farewell to his parents. The two came to a fork in the road, and parting was unavoidable.

Xiao Tao said to Wu Quan, "Elder brother Wu Quan, you want to persuade people to do good deeds, first of all you should treat yourself well. Please take good care of yourself. My mother told me, 留得青山在, 不怕没柴烧."[264]

Wu Quan said: "I will. Anyone who wants to 善始善终[265]should have a healthy body." He continued, "Xiao Tao, you are very young. You should value your time, study hard, and serve the society in the future. I

---

[262] 三 **sān** || **san** \ three. 天 **tiān** || **t'ien** \ day. 打 **dǎ** || **ta** \ catch. 鱼[魚] **yú** || **yü** \ fish. 打鱼: catch fish; fishing. 两 **liǎng** || **liang** \ two. 晒[曬] **shài** || **shai** \ dry in the sun. 网[網] **wǎng** || **wang** \ net; network. 三天打鱼, 两天晒网: Go fishing for three days and dry the nets for two days—work by fits and starts; work lazily and intermittently. (Idiom #262)

[263] 任 **rèn** || **jên** \ let; allow. 凭[憑] **píng** || **p'ing** \ no matter (what, how, etc.). 任凭: no matter (how, what, etc.). 风[風] **fēng** || **fêng** \ wind. 浪 **làng** || **lang** \ wave. 起 **qǐ** || **ch'i** \ rise. 稳[穩] **wěn** || **wên** \ steady; firm. 坐 **zuò** || **tso** \ sit. 钓[釣] **diào** || **tiao** \ fish with a hook and line. 鱼 **yú** || **yü** \ fish. 船 **chuán** || **ch'uan** \ boat; ship. 任凭风浪起, 稳坐钓鱼船: Sit tight in the fishing boat despite the rising winds and waves—persevere in the face of obstacles. (Idiom #263)

[264] 留 **liú** || **liu** \ remain; stay; keep. 得 **de** || **tê** \ <auxiliary word> (used after a verb or an adjective to express possibility or capability). 青 **qīng** || **ch'ing** \ blue or green. 山 **shān** || **shan** \ hill; mountain. 在 **zài** || **tsai** \ exist; be alive. 不 **bù** || **pu** \ no; not. 怕 **pà** || **p'a** \ fear; be afraid of. 没 **méi** || **mei** \ not have; be without. 柴 **chái** || **ch'ai** \ firewood. 烧[燒] **shāo** || **shao** \ burn. 留得青山在, 不怕没柴烧: As long as the green hills last, there will always be wood to burn—as long as one has good health, one can accomplish many things. (Idiom #264)

[265] 善 **shàn** || **shan** \ good. 始 **shǐ** || **shih** \ beginning; start; commencement. 终[終] **zhōng** || **chung** \ end; finish. 善始善终: Do well from beginning through to the end—do well all the time. (Idiom #265)

believe you 前途无量.[266]Please bear in mind: 有理走遍天下, 无理寸步难行.[267]Every step leaves its print, 千里之行, 始于足下."[268]

[266] 前 qián || ch'ien \ front; forward; ahead. 途 tú || t'u \ way; road; route. 前途: future; prospects. 无[無] wú || wu \ not have; there is not. 量 liàng || liang \ measure; amount; quantity. 无量: immeasurable; boundless. 前途无量: Have boundless prospects; have a bright future without limitation. (Idiom #266)

[267] 有 yǒu || yu \ have; there is; exist. 理 lǐ || li \ reason. 走 zǒu || tsou \ walk; go. 遍 biàn || pien \ all over; everywhere. 天 tiān || t'ien \ sky; heaven. 下 xià || hsia \ below; down; under; underneath. 天下: land under heaven—the world. 无[無] wú || wu \ not have; without. 寸 cùn || ts'un \ a unit of length (= 33.3 mm = 1.312 inch). 步 bù || pu \ step; pace. 寸步: a tiny step; a single step. 难 [難]nán || nan \ difficult; hard; hardly possible. 行 xíng || hsin \ go; travel. 有理走遍天下, 无理寸步难行: With justice on your side, you can go anywhere; without it, you can't take even one step—a just and fair person will be able to travel far and wide, but an unjust one will not go a great distance. (Idiom #267)

[268] 千 qiān || ch'ien \ thousand. 里 lǐ || li \ a Chinese unit of length (= 0.5 kilometer =~ 0.31 mile). 之 zhī || chih \ <auxiliary words> (used between an attribute and the word it modifies) 行 xíng || hsing \ go; travel; journey. 始 shǐ || shih \ beginning; start; commence. 于 yú || yü \ from; by. 足 zú || tsu \ foot. 下 xià || hsia \ below; down; under; underneath. 千里之行, 始于足下: A thousand-*li* (i.e. 500 kilometer, or ~310 mile) journey is started by taking the decisive first step. (Idiom #268)

§48

Xiao Tao and Wu Quan Parted Company

There were a broad way and a single-log bridge at their parting spot. Xiao Tao said to Wu Quan, "你走你的阳关道, 我走我的独木桥."[269] Wu Quan said, "Ok, let's 分道扬镳[270] from here," and walked away.

After cautiously crossing the bridge Xiao Tao started the first step, but his foot pain prevented him from walking. He had once foolishly cut his feet to fit his small shoes, and then 好了伤疤忘了疼.[271] Today the pain recurred.

---

269 你 nǐ || ni \ you. 走 zǒu || tsou \ walk; go; move. 的 de || tê \ <auxiliary word>. 你的: your; yours. 阳[陽] yáng || yang \ sun; sunny; openly. 关[關] guān || kuan \ mountain pass; closure. 道 dào || tao \ road, way, path; course. 阳关道: broad road; thoroughfare. 我 wǒ || wo \ I. 我的: my; mine. 独[獨] dú || tu \ only; single; alone. 木 mù || mu \ timber; wood. 桥[橋] qiáo || ch'iao \ bridge. 独木桥: single-plank (or single-log) bridge. 你走你的阳关道, 我走我的独木桥: You take the broad way, and I'll cross the single-log bridge—You go your way, and I'll go mine. (Idiom #269)

270 分 fēn || fên \ divide; separate; part. 道 dào || tao \ road, way, path; course. 扬[揚] yáng || yang \ raise. 镳[鑣] biāo || piao \ bit (of a bridle). 分道扬镳: Part company and each goes his own way. (Idiom #270)

271 好 hǎo || hao \ get well; good; fine. 了 le || lê \ <auxiliary word> (used after a verb to indicate the completion of an action) 伤[傷] shāng || shang \ wound; injury; hurt. 疤 bā || pa \ scar. 伤疤: scar. 忘 wàng || wang \ forget. 疼 téng || t'êng \ ache; pain; sore. 好了伤疤忘了疼: Forget the pain once the wound is healed; forget past suffering when the pain is gone—not learn a lesson from past mistake. (Idiom #271)

When he was feeling bewildered, an unexpected thing happened. The old white horse approached Xiao Tao again. It seemed that the horse had a bond with Xiao Tao.

有缘千里来相会,无缘对面不相逢.[272]The old horse bent down his body and let Xiao Tao ride on, and ran 风驰电掣.[273]

---

[272] 有 **yǒu** || yu \ have; there is; exist. 缘[緣] **yuán** || yüan \ predestined relationship; bond. 千 **qiān** || ch'ien \ thousand. 里 **lǐ** || li \ a Chinese unit of length (= 0.5 kilometer =~0.31 mile). 来[來] **lái** || lai \ come; arrive. 相 **xiāng** || hsiang \ each other; one another; mutually. 会[會] **huì** || hui \ get together; meet. 无[無] **wú** || wu \ not have; there is not; without. 对[對] **duì** || tui \ mutual; face to face; opposite. 面 **miàn** || mien \ face. 对面: right in front; face to face. 不 **bù** || pu \ no; not. 逢 **féng** || fêng \ meet; come upon. 有缘千里来相会, 无缘对面不相逢: When two people are fated to meet, they will meet across a thousand *li*; but when there is no fate, they will not meet though face to face. (Idiom #272)

[273] 风[風] **fēng** || fêng \ wind. 驰 [馳] **chí** || ch'ih \ speed; gallop. 电[電] **diàn** || tien \ electricity. 掣 **chè** || ch'ê \ flash past. 风驰电掣: Quick as wind and swift as lightning. (Idiom #273)

§49

The Kingdom of Yelong:
Too Big Territory for Dwarfs

The horse carried Xiao Tao on his back, and approached the Kingdom of Yelong.

The king of the state consistently 闭关锁国,[274]and therefore he was ignorant and ill informed. He 趾高气扬, 目中无人.[275]He was notorious for his 夜郎自大.[276]

Under his influence, all his subjects also believed that Yelong, which had only several villages, was among the biggest countries in the world.

---

[274] 闭[閉] bì || pi \ shut; close. 关[關] guān || kuan \ pass; customhouse. 锁[鎖] suǒ || so \ lock; lock up. 国[國] guó || kuo \ country; state; nation. 闭关锁国: Lock the gates of one country against the world. (Idiom #274)

[275] 趾 zhǐ || chih \ toe. 高 gāo || kao \ high; tall. 气[氣] qì || ch'i \ airs; air; gas. 扬 yáng || yang \ raise. 目 mù || mu \ eye. 中 zhōng || chung \ in; amid. 无[無] wú || wu \ not have; there is not; regardless of. 人 rén || jên \ person; people. 趾高气扬, 目中无人: Give oneself airs and look down upon everybody; think of oneself as above all others. (Idiom #275)

[276] 夜 yè || yeh \ night; evening. 郎 láng || lang \ an ancient official title; (used in forming nouns designating certain class of persons). 夜郎: an ancient small state in today's Guizhou Province, China. Its king considered his country was as big as the then Han Dynasty. 自 zì || tsǔ \ self; oneself. 大 dà || ta \ big; large; great. 自大: self-important; arrogant. 夜郎自大: Absurd arrogance of the King of Yelong; narrow-minded conceit—haughtiness. (Idiom #276)

The Kingdom of Yelong did not have much revenue, but the king 挥金如土.[277] For increasing revenue, he allowed people to drink and smoke harmful substances. Therefore, along with the decline of people's health was the decline of the state. Like 秋后的蚂蚱,[278] the existence of the Kingdom of Yelong would become history someday.

麻雀虽小, 五脏俱全.[279] The Kingdom of Yelong also had many ministries. An assistant minister in the Ministry of Foreign Affairs ordered Xiao Tao to kowtow to a portrait of the king. Xiao Tao refused, and therefore the official refused to let Xiao Tao enter the kingdom.

"Only dwarfs would think Yelong a big country. In a dwarf country, a pond might be regarded an ocean and a tadpole might be considered a whale!" Xiao Tao's good friend, the cricket chirped in his bamboo tube palace to comfort Xiao Tao.

---

[277] 挥 huī || hui \ scatter, disperse. 金 jīn || chin \ gold. 如 rú || ju \ like; as; can compare with. 土 tǔ || t'u \ dirt; soil; earth. 挥金如土: Throw money around like dirt; spend money like water. (Idiom #277)

[278] 秋 qiū || ch'iu \ autumn; fall. 后[後] hòu || hou \ after; later. 的 de || tê \ <auxiliary word> (used after an attribute) 蚂[螞] mā || ma \ some kinds of insects such as wasp; leech, ant, etc. 蚱 zhà || cha \ grasshopper. 蚂蚱 locust; grasshopper. 秋后的蚂蚱: A grasshopper at the end of autumn—coming to its end. (Idiom #278)

[279] 麻 má || ma \ spotty; pockmarked. 雀 què || ch'üeh \ small bird; sparrow. 麻雀: (house) sparrow. 虽[雖] suī || sui \ though; although; even if. 小 xiǎo || hsiao \ small; little; petty. 五 wǔ || wu \ five. 脏[臟] zàng || tsang \ internal organs of the body. 五脏: the five internal organs (heart, liver, spleen, lungs and kidneys). 俱 jù || chü \ all; complete. 全 quán || ch'uan \ complete; full. 俱全: complete in all varieties. 麻雀虽小, 五脏俱全: The sparrow may be small but it has all the vital organs—small yet complete. (Idiom #279)

§50

The Dukedom of Shamelessness:
Fulsome Praises

The old white horse carried Xiao Tao and left the Kingdom of Yelong. They then unwittingly entered the Dukedom of Shamelessness. A hippopotamus in the town moat was the duke. In the dukedom everyone was thick-skinned and had the nerve to flatter their leader.

The hippo duke snored thunderously in the town moat. People praised, "This nice melody should be only heard in heaven, but we are lucky enough to enjoy it here!"

The hippo exhaled in the moat and produced a lot of bubbles. People said, "Gee, our duke is doing underwater hard work, and taking the trouble to purify the moat." Someone flattered proudly, "See, our leader made so many colorful bubbles that include all our beautiful dreams!"

The daughter of the 青面獠牙[280]duke, a little hippo, whispered to Xiao Tao, "I have features that can 沉鱼落雁, 闭月羞花.[281] You are a prince on white horse. We are a heavenly made match!"

---

[280] 青 qīng || ch'ing \ blue or green. 面 miàn || mien \ face. 獠 liáo || liao \ fierce. 牙 yá || ya \ tooth. 獠牙: long, sharp, protruding teeth. 青面獠牙: Green-faced and long-toothed—frightening in appearance; have monster-like features. (Idiom #280)

[281] 沉 chén || ch'ên \ sink; keep down; lower. 鱼[魚] yú || yü \ fish. 落 luò || lo \ fall; drop; go down; set. 雁 yàn || yen \ wild goose. 闭[閉] bì || pi \ obstruct; stop up; shut; close. 月 yuè || yüeh \ the moon. 羞 xiū || hsiu \ shy; bashful; feel ashamed or embarrassed. 花 huā || hua \ flower; bloom. 沉鱼落雁, 闭月羞花: (Of feminine beauty) makes fish sink and birds fall,

Xiao Tao broke out into a cold sweat. The little girl hippo said, "Why do you 前怕狼, 后怕虎?[282]We, not our parents can decide our 终身大事."[283]

Xiao Tao said, "This is your 一厢情愿.[284]I am only twelve years old, and I am afraid of small animals such as caterpillars and big animals such as hippos."

The girl hippo said with a grin, "An ugly caterpillar will grow into a beautiful butterfly."

"But a small hippo can never become a swan," Xiao Tao argued.

Xiao Tao 快马加鞭[285]and left the Dukedom of Shamelessness. He didn't forget shouting loudly to the girl hippo, "I ride on a white horse, but I am not a prince at all!"

---

and has looks that can outshine the moon and put the flowers to shame—of great beauty. (Idiom #281)

[282] 前 qián || ch'ien \ front; ahead; forward. 怕 pà || p'a \ fear; be afraid of. 狼 láng || lang \ wolf. 后[後] hòu || hou \ back; behind; rear. 虎 hǔ || hu \ tiger. 前怕狼,后怕虎: Fear wolves ahead and tigers behind—to be afraid of many things. (Idiom #282)

[283] 终[終] zhōng || chung \ whole; entire. 身 shēn || shên \ body; life. 终身: lifelong; all one's life. 大 dà || ta \ big; large; great. 事 shì || shih \ matter; affair. 终身大事: The most important matter in one's life (usually referring to marriage). (Idiom #283)

[284] 一 yī || i \ one; single. 厢[廂] xiāng || hsiang \ side. 情 qíng || ch'ing \ feeling; affection; sentiment. 愿[願] yuàn || yüan \ hope; wish; desire. 情愿: be willing to. 一厢情愿: One-sided longing; one's own wishful thinking. (Idiom #284)

[285] 快 kuài || k'uai \ fast; quick; rapid; swift. 马[馬] mǎ || ma \ horse. 加 jiā || chia \ add; plus. 鞭 biān || pien \ whip; lash; flog. 快马加鞭: Spur on the flying horse—hastily; rapidly. (Idiom #285)

"You are 可望而不可即 . . ."[286]On horseback, Xiao Tao heard the little hippo's sob.

"Poor and silly girl," he sighed for her 异想天开.[287]

286　可 kě || k'ê \ can; may. 望 wàng || wang \ gaze into the distance; hope; expect. 而 ér || êrh \ but; and yet; while on the other hand. 不 bù || pu \ no; not. 即 jí || chi \ approach; reach; be near. 可望而不可即: Within sight but beyond reach—unobtainable. (Idiom #286)

287　异[異] yì || i \ strange; unusual; extraordinary. 想 xiǎng || hsiang \ think; suppose; consider; want to. 天 tiān \\ t'ien \ sky; heaven. 开[開] kāi || k'ai \ open. 异想天开: Have the wildest fantasy; indulge in a far-fetched dream. (Idiom #287)

§51

The Valley of Hate:
Brothers Fought Tooth & Nail over a Trifle

Xiao Tao looked ahead and saw flames lighting up the sky. He didn't know what had happened and stopped to ask about it.

He learned that this place was the Valley of Hate, and a Creek of Hate flowed through the valley. The governess of the valley was a huge crab who printed a skeleton on her back shell as her totem. She acted like an overlord, 横行霸道[288]and did whatever she wished. In addition, she 惟恐天下不乱,[289]and sowed hatred and stirred up fights wherever and whenever possible.

---

[288] 横 héng || heng \ violently; fiercely. 行 xíng || hsing \ go; travel. 横行: run wild; run amuck; be on a rampage. 霸 bà || pa \ tyrannical 道 dào || tao \ doctrine; principle; way; road, path; course. 霸道: rule by force; unreasonable. 横行霸道: Go on a rampage; terrorize; dictate; oppress. (Idiom #288)

[289] 惟 wéi || wei \ only. 恐 kǒng || k'ung \ fear; be afraid of. 天 tiān || t'ien \ sky; heaven. 下 xià || hsia \ below; down; under; underneath. 天下: land under heaven—the world. 不 bù || pu \ no; not. 乱[亂] luàn || luan \ disorder; chaos; riot; turmoil. 惟恐天下不乱: Be eager for nothing other than nationwide chaos; love chaos and troubles. (Idiom #289)

On that very day, in Li's family, two brothers quarreled over a 鸡毛蒜皮[290]affair, 祸起萧墙,[291]and they fought tooth and nail. The younger brother 李五(Li Wu, lǐ wǔ || li wu) set a fire and burnt his elder brother's woods, and the elder brother 李四 (Li Si, lǐ sì || li ssǔ) used a knife to threaten Li Wu and hurt his shoulder.

Li Wu's friend did not dissuade him from arson, on the other hand, they 火上浇油.[292]Li Si's friends did try to put out the fire, but only 杯水车薪.[293]Many valuable things 付之一炬.[294]On the opposite bank of the Creek of Hate, people just 隔岸观火. [295]

---

[290] 鸡[雞] jī || chi \ chicken. 毛 máo || mao \ hair; feather. 蒜 suàn || suan \ garlic. 皮 pí || p'i \ skin; leather. 鸡毛蒜皮: Chicken feathers and garlic skins—small and insignificant matters. (Idiom #290)

[291] 祸[禍] huò || huo \ misfortune; disaster; catastrophe. 起 qǐ || ch'i \ start; begin; arise; rise. 萧[蕭] xiāo || hsiao \ desolate; dreary. 墙[牆] qiáng || ch'iang \ wall. 萧墙: the screen wall facing the gate of a Chinese house. 祸起萧墙: Trouble arises behind the walls of the home—trouble arises inside the home. (Idiom #291)

[292] 火 huǒ || huo \ fire. 上 shang || shang \ (used after a noun) on. 浇[澆] jiāo || chiao \ pour. 油 yóu || yu \ oil. 火上浇油: Pour oil on the flames—to make matters worse. (Idiom #292)

[293] 杯 bēi || pei \ cup; mug. 水 shuǐ || shui \ water. 车[車] chē || ch'ê \ vehicle. 薪 xīn || hsin \ firewood; fuel. 杯水车薪: Trying to put out raging flames on cartload of firewood with a cup of water—an utterly insufficient action. (Idiom #293)

[294] 付 fù || fu \ turn (or hand) over to; commit to; pay. 之 zhī || chih \ <pronoun> used as object. 一 yī || i \ one; single. 炬 jù || chü \ torch; fire. 付之一炬: Commit to the fire; succumb to the flames. (Idiom #294)

[295] 隔 gé || kê \ be at a distance from; be apart from; separate. 岸 àn || an \ bank; shore; coast. 观[觀] guān || kuan \ look at; watch; observe. 火 huǒ || huo \ fire. 隔岸观火: Watch a fire from the other bank of the river—watch the other's suffering from afar. (Idiom #295)

Xiao Tao disliked 各人自扫门前雪,[296]and he 见义勇为.[297]Seeing a big bunch of jute near a townhouse was setting on fire, he took out his knife and 快刀斩乱麻.[298]The fire went out, but before long it 死灰复燃.[299]Xiao Tao and the white horse stepped on the burning jute repeatedly, and eventually made the diehard fire die out.

"Be careful, 多行不义必自毙.[300]Remember the saying of 玩火自焚!"[301]Xiao Tao warned Li Wu while leaving the Valley of Hate.

[296] 各 gè || kê \ each; every. 人 rén || jên \ person; people. 自 zì || tsŭ\ self; one's own. 扫[掃] sǎo || sao \ sweep; clear away. 门[門] mén || mên \ door; gate. 前 qián || ch'ien \ front; forward; ahead. 雪 xuě || hsüeh \ snow. 各人自扫门前雪: Each one sweeps the snow from his own doorstep—each person only minds his own business. (Idiom #296)

[297] 见[見] jiàn || chien \ see; catch sight of. 义[義] yì || i \ justice; righteousness; rightful; just. 勇 yǒng || yung \ brave; valiant; courageous. 为[為] wéi || wei \ do; act. 见义勇为: See what is right and have the courage to do it; have the courage to stand up for what is just and right. (Idiom #297)

[298] 快 kuài || k'uai \ sharp; fast; quick. 刀 dāo || tao \ knife; sword. 斩[斬] zhǎn || chan \ chop; cut; behead. 乱[亂] luàn || luan \ messy; tangled; in disorder; in confusion. 麻 má || ma \ a general term for hemp, flax, jute, etc. 快刀斩乱麻: Cut a tangled skein of jute with a sharp knife—solve a complex problem quickly; get to the root of the problem. (Idiom #298)

[299] 死 sǐ || ssŭ\ die; be dead. 灰 huī || hui \ ash; cinders; dust. 复[復] fù || fu \ again. 燃 rán || jan \ burn; ignite; light. 死灰复燃: Dying cinders glowing again—rekindle. (Idiom #299)

[300] 多 duō || to \ many; much; more. 行 xíng || hsing \ do; perform. 不 bù || pu \ no; not. 义[義] yì || i \ justice; rightfulness; righteous; just. 必 bì || pi \ certainly; surely; must; have to. 自 zì || tsŭ\ self; one's own. 毙[斃] bì || pi \ die; get killed. 多行不义必自毙: He who is always unjust is fated to meet a bad end. (Idiom #300)

[301] 玩 wán || wan \ play; have fun; amuse. 火 huǒ || huo \ fire. 自 zì || tsŭ\ self; one's own. 焚 fén || fên \ burn. 玩火自焚: Whoever plays with fire will be destroyed by fire. (Idiom #301)

§52

The Cave of Reverse:
"Sky Is Underfoot and Earth Is Overhead"

Xiao Tao then made a detour to the Cave of Reverse.

The monarch of cave dwellers was a huge vampire bat. Most subjects were bats too. Big bats were bloodthirsty and ranked high. Small bats were all vegetarians. Mid-sized bats could taste blood through eating mosquitoes, provided that these mosquitoes had just sucked blood prior to entering the bats' stomachs.

Bats were used to hanging themselves up side down and seeing things down side up. They considered nights as days and days as nights, because they worked at night and slept at daytime.

The monarch had very bad eyesight, but his one sentence told all: "The color of snow is black, and the color of coal is white." He was an expert of 颠倒黑白[302] and 混淆视听.[303] Anyone who dared to say the opposite would be put into a cage and starved to death. As a result, in that cave everything was reversed.

---

[302] 颠 diān || tien \ turn over. 倒 dào || tao \ upside down. 颠倒: put (or turn) upside down 黑 hēi || hei \ black; dark. 白 bái || pai \ white; clear; blank. 颠倒黑白: Confound black with white; confuse the truth; distort reality. (Idiom #302)

[303] 混 hùn || hun \ mix; confuse. 淆 xiáo || hsiao \ confuse; mix. 混淆: confuse; mix up. 视 shì || shih \ look at; watch. 听[聽] tīng || t'ing \ listen; hear. 视听: seeing and hearing; what is seen and heard. 混淆视听: Mislead the public; confuse public viewpoint. (Idiom #303)

In winter, a quilt of snow covered the ground, but for bats in the Cave of Reverse, they just felt someone had paved asphalt beneath the sky. In summer, everyone felt hot, but they felt icy cold; at least they should pretend to feel so in order to keep safety.

The general judge of the Cave of Reverse had been a huge bee, and the bee was just and could distinguish right from wrong. However, the monarch disliked the bee and appointed a huge fly to replace the bee.

According to the new judge, shit was clean and soap was dirty; garbage such as rotten pork was very pretty and fragrant and therefore edible; on the other hand, carnation flowers were very ugly and stinky and therefore no fly approached them.

The funny thing was, all subjects in the Cave of Reverse thought their princess, a young bat was 如花似玉,[304]and could 不费吹灰之力[305]win the championship of a coming Miss Wonderland Pageant.

Xiao Tao laughed until he was bent forwards and backwards on his horseback, and told them 骄兵必败.[306]

---

[304] 如 rú || ju \ like; as; as if; can compare with. 花 huā || hua \ flower; bloom. 似 sì || ssǔ\ similar; like; seem. 玉 yù || yü \ jade. 如花似玉: As beautiful as flowers and jade—(of a woman) young and beautiful. (Idiom #304)

[305] 不 bù || pu \ no; not. 费[費] fèi || fei \ cost; spend. 吹 chuī || ch'ui \ blow; puff. 灰 huī || hui \ ash; dust. 之 zhī || chih \ <auxiliary word> (used between an attribute and the word it modifies) 力 lì || li \ force; power; strength. 不费吹灰之力: Easier than blowing off dust; extremely easy—a piece of cake. (Idiom #305)

[306] 骄[驕] jiāo || chiao \ proud; arrogant; conceited. 兵 bīng || ping \ soldier. 必 bì || pi \ certainly; surely; must; have to. 败[敗] bài || pai \ fail; be defeated; lose; defeat. 骄兵必败: The self-conceited troops are destined to fail—pride goes before destruction. (Idiom #306)

§53

The Marshland of Hypocrisy: Honey-mouthed & Dagger-hearted

Xiao Tao's last stop was the Marshland of Hypocrisy. The ruler there was a 100-year old snake monster.

The authority of that marshland told people that their ancestors once had been stuck in the marsh, and the snake twined and pulled them out. They honored the snake monster as their savior and worshipped him as a supreme deity. People believed that the 口蜜腹剑,[307]老奸巨猾[308]snake would bring happiness to them, and the marshland was indeed the nicest place in the world to live.

---

[307] 口 kǒu || k'ou \ mouth. 蜜 mì || mi \ honey; sweet. 腹 fù || fu \ belly; abdomen; stomach. 剑[劍] jiàn || chien \ sword; sabre. 口蜜腹剑: Honey-mouthed and dagger-hearted; honey on one's lips and poison in one's heart. (Idiom #307)

[308] 老 lǎo || lao \ old; aged. 奸 jiān || chien \ wicked; evil; treacherous. 巨 jù || chü \ huge; tremendous; gigantic. 猾 huá || hua \ cunning; crafty; sly. 老奸巨猾: An experienced rogue; a sly old fox; a deceitful and scheming individual. (Idiom #308)

People in every family apparently were starving, but they kept the principle of 家丑不可外扬,[309]and still 打肿脸充胖子.[310]Actually, people were required to tell lies; on the other hand, telling truth would be punished.

The snake monster liked to watch his subjects fight. He always 蛊惑人心,[311]and called on his subjects to fight each other. He gave big promotion to the winner of the fighting. As for those losers, they were just 打入十八层地狱.[312]

A witch waved smilingly to Xiao Tao and used her 三寸不烂之舌[313]to persuade him to visit the Marshland of Hypocrisy as an honored guest.

---

[309] 家 jiā || chia \ family; household; home. 丑[醜] chǒu || ch'ou \ disgrace; ugly. 不 bù || pu \ no; not. 可 kě || k'ê \ can; may. 外 wài || wai \ outer; outward; outside. 扬[揚] yáng || yang \ spread. 家丑不可外扬: The disgrace of a family should never be spread outside—do not air one's dirty laundry in public. (Idiom #309)

[310] 打 dǎ || ta \ beat; strike; hit; knock. 肿[腫] zhǒng || chung \ swollen. 脸[臉] liǎn || lien \ face. 充 chōng || ch'ung \ pretend to be ; pose as. 胖 pàng || p'ang \ fat; stout; plump. 子 zi || tsǔ \ (noun suffix) 胖子: fat person; fatty. 打肿脸充胖子: Slap one's face until it is swollen in an effort to look strong and well-built; pretend everything being well when the opposite is true. (Idiom #310)

[311] 蛊[蠱] gǔ || ku \ a legendary venomous insect. 惑 huò || huo \ delude; mislead. 人 rén || jên \ person; people. 心 xīn || hsin \ heart; mind; feeling; intention. 人心: popular feeling; public feeling; the will of people. 蛊惑人心: Confuse public feeling and poison people's hearts; play up on people's emotions and prejudices. (Idiom #311)

[312] 打 dǎ || ta \ beat; strike; hit. 入 rù || ju \ go into. 十 shí || shih \ ten. 八 bā || pa \ eight. 十八 eighteen. 层[層] céng || ts'êng \ floor; storey. 地 dì || ti \ the earth; land; ground. 狱[獄] yù || yü \ prison; jail. 地狱: hell; inferno. 打入十八层地狱: Banish to the lowest depths (i.e. the eighteenth floor) of hell—convict to eternal damnation. (Idiom #312)

[313] 三 sān || san \ three. 寸 cùn || ts'un \ a unit of length (= 33.3 mm = 1.312 inch). 不 bù || pu \ no; not. 烂[爛] làn || lan \ rot. 之 zhī || chih \ <auxiliary word> (used between an attribute and the word it modifies) 舌 shé || shê \ tongue. 三寸不烂之舌: A lithesome tongue; an eloquent tongue. (Idiom #313)

135

However, Xiao Tao learned that this year a huge poisonous scorpion, which had stung all its rivals and poisoned their blood won the laurel of "hero" in the Marshland of Hypocrisy. And the "hero" was fond of stinging little boys.

In that marshland everyone 心怀叵测[314]and 假仁假义[315]. Xiao Tao saw a cat killed a mouse, but 猫哭老鼠[316]in the bordering area of the marshland. In addition, he heard that in the marshland in New Year season the yellow weasels, which were addicted to eating chickens, often played 黄鼠狼给鸡拜年[317]before taking the chickens as delicious dinner.

To go or not to go to such a place where 人人自危?[318]For an adventurous child it was a big question. Xiao Tao 进退两难.[319]

---

[314] 心 xīn || hsin \ heart; feeling; intention. 怀[懷] huái || huai \ harbor; have; bosom. 叵 pǒ || p'o \ impossible. 测[測] cè || ts'ê \ survey; fathom; measure. 叵测: unfathomable; unpredictable. 心怀叵测: Have unfathomable schme; harbor evil intentions. (Idiom #314)

[315] 假 jiǎ || chia \ false; fake. 仁 rén || jên \ benevolence; kindheartedness; humanity. 义[義] yì || i \ justice; righteousness. 假仁假义: Feigned benevolence and righteousness; hypocrisy. (Idiom #315)

[316] 猫 māo || mao \ cat. 哭 kū || k'u \ cry; weep. 老 lǎo || lao \ <used as a prefix> (in certain names of animals) 鼠 shǔ || shu \ mouse; rat. 猫哭老鼠: The cat weeping over the killed mouse—shed fake tears. (Idiom #316)

[317] 黄 huáng || huang \ yellow. 鼠 shǔ || shu \ mouse; rat. 狼 láng || lang \ wolf. 黄鼠狼: yellow weasel. 给 gěi || kei \ <preposition> (used to introduce the recipient of an action) 鸡[雞] jī || chi \ chicken. 拜 bài || pai \ do obeisance; make a courtesy call; congratulate (on a certain occasion) 年 nián || nien \ year; New Year. 拜年: pay a New Year visit (or call); wish somebody a Happy New Year. 黄鼠狼给鸡拜年: The weasel goes to pay his respects to the chicken—having hidden and sinister objectives. (Idiom #317)

[318] 人 rén || jên \ person; people. 人人: everybody; everyone. 自 zì || tsǔ \ self; one's own. 危 wēi || wei \ danger; peril. 人人自危: Everyone finds himself in peril; everyone feels insecure. (Idiom #318)

[319] 进[進] jìn || chin \ advance; move forward. 退 tuì || t'ui \ move back; retreat; withdraw. 两[兩] liǎng || liang \ two; both. 难[難] nán || nan \ difficult; hard. 进退两难: Find it difficult to advance or to retreat; be stuck between a rock and a hard place—a dilemma. (Idiom #319)

Luckily the old white horse and Xiao Tao 心有灵犀一点通.[320]The horse was so clever that he quietly and swiftly walked along the edge of the marshland and carried Xiao Tao to leave the troublesome place.

---

[320] 心 xīn || hsin \ heart; feeling; intention. 有 yǒu || yu \ have; there is; exist. 灵[靈] líng || ling \ quick; clever; sharp; spirit. 犀 xī || hsi \ rhinoceros. 灵犀: magic horn (i.e. rhinoceros horn mentioned in classical text as having a high sensibility) 一 yī || i \ one; single. 点[點] diǎn || tien \ touch on very briefly; dot stroke. 通 tōng || t'ung \ connected understand; know. 心有灵犀一点通: Hearts which beat in unison are connected—know each other very well. (Idiom #320)

§54

A Bolt from the Blue

路遥知马力.[321]Xiao Tao finally arrived at his long-missed home. But both Xiao Tao and the white horse were 筋疲力尽.[322]Xiao Tao's little companion, the cricket, was still alive, but he was very hungry and thirsty. Xiao Tao served the cricket first.

Mom and dad were overjoyed. Sisters Da Niu and Er Niu were smiling all over, and asked about this and that. But dad was lying on a bed and could not get up.

Xiao Tao asked why dad could not get up. Dad said, "天有不测风云, 人有旦夕祸福.[323]This is not at all surprising."

---

[321] 路 lù || lu \ road; path; way. 遥 yáo || yao \ distant; remote; far. 知 zhī || chih \ know; realize; be aware of. 马[馬] mǎ || ma \ horse. 力 lì || li \ power; strength; stamina; ability. 路遥知马力, (often followed by 日久见人心): Distance reveals a horse's stamina, (and time discloses a person's heart. 日 rì || jih \ day; time. 久 jiǔ || chiu \ for a long time. 见[見] jiàn || chien \ see;. 人 rén || jên \ person; people. 心 xīn || hsin \ heart.) (Idiom #321)

[322] 筋 jīn || chin \ tendon; veins that stand out under the skin. 疲 pí || p'i \ tired; weary; exhausted. 力 lì || li \ power; strength; ability. 尽[盡] jìn || chin \ exhausted; finished. 筋疲力尽: Exhausted; very tired; run down. (Idiom #322)

[323] 天 tiān || t'ien \ sky; heaven. 有 yǒu || yu \ have; there is; exist. 不 bù || pu \ no; not. 测[測] cè || ts'ê \ survey; fathom; measure. 不测: unpredictable. 风[風] fēng || fêng \ wind. 云[雲] yún || yün \ cloud. 风云: wind and cloud—a stormy or unstable situation. 人 rén || jên \ person; people. 旦 dàn || tan \ dawn; daybreak; day. 夕 xī || hsi \ sunset; evening; night. 祸[禍] huò || huo \ misfortune; disaster; calamity. 福 fú || fu \ good fortune;

Mom said, "It's all my fault. Before, your dad said here was pain and there was pain, I thought he was 无病呻吟,"[324]she then whispered to Xiao Tao, "but actually your dad already 病入膏肓.[325]病急乱投医,[326]I asked many doctors for help, but your dad is still not on the mend."

For Xiao Tao, seeing his dad in such a state was 晴天霹雳.[327]He asked dad which disease he had got, but dad did not answer.

Mom said, "讳疾忌医[328]is not good, but doctors really do not know with certainty which disease your dad has."

Dad said, "冰冻三尺，非一日之寒.[329]I have got the sickness since you left home."

---

blessing; happiness. 天有不测风云，人有旦夕祸福: Just as the weather can be unpredictable, life also holds many unexpected events. (Idiom #323)

[324] 无[無] wú || wu \ not have; there is not; without. 病 bìng || ping \ ill; sick; disease. 呻 shēn || shên \ groan. 吟 yín || yin \ chant; recite. 呻吟: groan; moan. 无病呻吟: Moan and groan without being sick; pretend to suffer from an illness. (Idiom #324)

[325] 病 bìng || ping \ ill; sick; disease. 入 rù || ju \ go into; enter. 膏 gāo || kao \ paste; cream. 肓 huàng || huang \ (ancient, of human body) the part between heart and diaphragm. 膏肓: the vital organs. 病入膏肓: The disease has attacked the vital organs—incurable; beyond remedy. (Idiom #325)

[326] 病 bìng || ping \ ill; sick; disease. 急 jí || chi \ urgent; pressing; anxious; worry. 乱[亂] luàn || luan \ in disorder; in a mess; in confusion; disorder. 投 tóu || t'ou \ go to; join. 医[醫] yī || i \ doctor (of medicine); cure; treat. 投医: seek medical advice; go to a doctor. 病急乱投医: Turn to any doctor one can find when critically sick—seek out any possible solutions when in a desperate situation. (Idiom #326)

[327] 晴 qíng || ch'ing \ fine; clear. 天 tiān || t'ien \ sky. 晴天: fine day; sunny day. 霹 pī || p'i \ clap of thunder. 雳[靂] lì || li \ clap of thunder. 霹雳: thunderbolt; thunderclap. 晴天霹雳: A bolt from the blue; a shock. (Idiom #327)

[328] 讳[諱] huì || hui \ avoid as taboo; forbidden word; taboo. 疾 jí || chi \ disease; sickness; illness. 忌 jì || chi \ fear; dread; abstain from. 医[醫] yī || i \ doctor (of medicine); cure; treat. 讳疾忌医: Hide one's illness for fear of treatment—hide one's weakness for fear of other's ridicule or disapproval. (Idiom #328)

[329] 冰 bīng || ping \ ice. 冻[凍] dòng || tung \ freeze. 三 sān || san \ three. 尺 chǐ || ch'ih \ a unit of length (= 0.333 meter = 1.093 foot). 三尺: 3 chǐ

139

§55

"Bitter Medicine Cures Sickness,
Unpleasant Advice Benefits Conduct"

Xiao Tao delivered a spoon of medicine to dad, but dad refused, complaining about its bitterness.

Mom said, "良药苦口利于病，忠言逆耳利于行.[330]Your sickness will be cured only if the medicine is taking effect. How can you be like a child, afraid of bitterness?"

Dad suddenly sat up and said, "My disease was nothing other than worries. Mental worries cannot be cured by medicine. I thought my son's leaving without saying goodbye was the result of an evildoer's seduction.

(= 1 meter = 3.281 feet). 非 fēi || fei \ not; no. 一 yī || i \ one; single. 日 rì || jih \ day. 之 zhī || chih \ <auxiliary word> (used to connect the modifier and the word it modifies) 寒 hán || han \ cold. 冰冻三尺, 非一日之寒: It takes more than one cold day for the river or lake to freeze three *chi* deep—the problem has been developing for quite a while. (Idiom #329)

[330] 良 liáng || liang \ good; fine. 药[藥]yào || yao \ medicine; drug; remedy. 苦 kǔ || k'u \ bitter. 口 kǒu || k'ou \ mouth. 利 lì || li \ benefit; profit. 于 yú || yü \ at; in. 利于: be good for; be of advantage to; benefit. 病 bìng || ping \ ill; sick; disease. 忠 zhōng || chung \ loyal; devoted; honest. 言 yán || yen \ speech; word. 逆 nì || ni \ contrary; counter; go against. 耳 ěr || êrh \ ear. 行 xíng || hsing \ behavior; conduct. 良药苦口利于病, 忠言逆耳利于行: Bitter medicine, though revolting to the mouth, is beneficial for health; honest advice, though offensive to the ear, is good for behavior—hearing the truth may be hard, but it is good for a person in a long run . (Idiom #330)

140

I only reared him but did not educate him, and this was my fault. Now he is back, just like 枯木逢春,[331]my sickness is naturally healed!"

Everyone felt relieved and beamed with joy.

---

[331] 枯 kū || k'u \ (of a plant, etc.) withered; (of a well, river, etc.) dried up. 木 mù || mu \ tree; timber; wood. 逢 féng || fêng \ meet; come upon. 春 chūn || ch'un \ spring. 枯木逢春: Spring comes to the withered tree—have renewed life. (Idiom #331)

§56

Having a Cat Was for Catching Mice, Not for Looking Nice

Xiao Tao had a sound sleep that night. However, mice awaked him.

Mom said mice recently were rampant in the house, and they needed a cat.

Da Niu wanted a white cat, since white cat looked nice; but Er Nir liked a black cat, because black cat looked nicer.

Xiao Tao said: "不管白猫黑猫, 能捉老鼠就是好猫."[332]

Mom said, "Xiao Tao is right. Cats with different colors are all able to catch mice in darkness."

They soon got a leopard cat with spotted faint brown hairs. All mice 胆战心惊,[333] and ran away.

---

[332] 不 bù || pu \ no; not. 管 guǎn || kuan \ manage; run; be in charge of; take care of. 不管: no matter (what, how, etc.); regardless of. 白 bái || pai \ white. 猫 māo || mao \ cat. 黑 hēi || hei \ black. 能 néng || nêng \ can; be able to; be capable of. 捉 zhuō || cho \ catch; capture; clutch. 老 lǎo || lao \ <used as a prefix> (in certain names of animals). 鼠 shǔ || shu \ mouse; rat. 就 jiù || chiu \ in that case; then; just; simply. 是 shì || shih \ be. 好 hǎo || hao \ good; fine; nice. 不管白猫黑猫, 能捉老鼠就是好猫: No matter white cat or black cat, as long as it can catch mice it must be a good cat—appearance does not matter as much as one's inner nature.. (Idiom #332)

[333] 胆 dǎn || tan \ courage; guts. 战[戰] zhàn || chan \ shiver; tremble. 心 xīn || hsin \ heart; feeling; intention. 惊[驚] jīng || ching \ be frightened; shock; alarm. 胆战心惊: Tremble with fright. shake with fear. (Idiom #333)

Next morning, dad said to Xiao Tao: "光阴似箭.[334]You went out for quite long time, and you must have learned a lot."

一言难尽.[335]Xiao Tao concisely told his adventure stories one by one.

After hearing his son's stories, dad said, "So, you entered both human and animal societies?"

"Yes."

"管中窥豹, 可见一斑.[336]Can you tell us what is the difference between the human and the animal societies?"

Xiao Tao thought for a while, and shook his head, "Sorry. I can't tell."

"It might be too difficult for a twelve-year old boy," said dad, "Well, I think animals are much more frank and sincere than humans. For instance, a lion or a bear when hungry will pounce on a human and eat him, but it never tries to find an excuse or cook up a 'theory' explaining away its beastliness."

---

[334] 光 guāng || kuang \ light; ray; brightness; luster. 阴[陰] yīn || yin \ overcast; shade. 光阴: time. 似 sì || ssǔ\ similar; like; seem. 箭 jiàn || chien \ arrow. 光阴似箭: Time flies like an arrow; time passes quickly. (Idiom #334)

[335] 一 yī || i \ one; single. 言 yán || yen \ word; talk. 难[難] nán || nan \ difficult; hard. 尽[盡] jìn || chin \ exhausted; finished. 一言难尽: It's hard to tell the whole story in a few words—it's a long story. (Idiom #335)

[336] 管 guǎn || kuan \ tube; pipe. 中 zhōng || chung \ center; middle; in; among. 窥 kuī || k'uei \ peep; spy. 豹 bào || pao \ leopard; panther. 可 kě || k'ê \ can; may. 见 jiàn || chien \ see; catch sight of. 一 yī || i \ one; single. 斑 bān || pan \ spot. 管中窥豹, 可见一斑: Peep at one spot on a leopard through a pipe and you can visualize the whole beast; having seen one, you've seen it all. (Idiom #336)

§57

The Complication of Simple Math

Mom interrupted dad, and said, "Xiao Tao, you missed a lot of school lessons and homework. I'm worried about it."

Dad said, "Let me test you a little to see if you can quickly make it up or not."

"Yes, please set a question and quiz me."

"You met a fisherman twice, and so I test you a math problem related to fishing. A fisherman went out to fix his fishing fork. After returning home, his wife asked how many fish he had got. He said: '6 fish without head, 9 without tail, and 8 had only half body.' Tell me how many fish he actually got."

Xiao Tao carefully calculated the applied arithmetic: 6 fish without head could only count as 3 fish, 9 without tail could be counted as 4 ½ fish and 8 half body should be 4 fish. 3 + 4 ½ + 4 = 11½. "Eleven and half," shouted Xiao Tao.

"Not right!" Da Niu said. "'6' after beheading becomes '0,' '9' after cutting tail turns to '0' too, and '8' is composed of two '0's."

Er Niu shouted, "0 + 0 + 0 = 0. The fisherman didn't get any fish at all!"

Dad said, "The fisherman went out to fix his fork. Now that he did not go fishing, of course he got no fish at all!"

Xiao Tao complained, "This is not a quiz. It is just a joke!"

"Anyhow, you should listen to the question clearly, and think carefully. Only through this way you can get the right answer." Mom continued, " 蜻蜓点水[337]won't work. For instance, a fish without head did not have

---

[337] 蜻 qīng || ch'ing \ dragonfly. 蜓 tíng || t'ing \ dragonfly. 蜻蜓: dragonfly. 点[點] diǎn || tien \ touch upon. 水 shuǐ || shui \ water. 蜻蜓点水: Like

a mouth, how could it bite the hook? A fish without tail couldn't swim, and half body fish must be already dead, how could they be greedy for the bait?" All of them smiled.

"Applying math must be reasonable," said dad.

a dragonfly skimming the surface of water—pass over something swiftly and lightly. (Idiom #337)

§58

The Longest Individual Word in English

Dad went on, "To learn a foreign language is important. It's a pity that your mom and I know nothing about any foreign language. You should at least understand English."

Xiao Tao said, "English should be easier than math."

"Let me test you," said Da Niu. She took a piece of paper with "B," "I" and "O" on it, and let Xiao Tao to read. Xiao Tao said, "This is too easy. '13,' '1' and '0.'"

Da Niu said, "You got English letters and Arabic numerals 混为一谈,[338] and how could it be right? 'BIO' is an English word, which means 'biography,' usually a very brief biography. '13,' '1' and '0' are numbers. They are 风马牛不相及."[339]

Er Niu said to her sister. "Da Niu, I'd like also to test you. Which individual word is the longest one in English?"

Da Niu thought for quite a while, and said, "It seems to me the word 'acknowledgement,' and there are fifteen letters in it."

"Incorrect!" Said Er Niu.

Dar Niu said, "Let me look it up in a dictionary."

---

[338] 混 hùn || hun \ mix; confuse; jumble. 为 wéi || wei \ become; be. 一 yī || i \ one. 谈[談]tán || t'an \ talk; chat; discuss. 混为一谈: Jumble (or lump) things together; confuse one thing with another; make a jumble of things. (Idiom #338)

[339] 风[風] fēng || fêng \ wind. 马 [馬] mǎ || ma \ horse. 牛 niú || niu \ ox; cow. 不 bù || pu \ no; not. 相 xiāng || hsiang \ each other; one another; mutually. 及 jí || chi \ reach; come up to. 风马牛不相及: Have absolutely no relation to each other; completely disparate. (Idiom #339)

"You don't need a dictionary, because the longest word is not in it."

"How can it be?"

Er Niu said, "Let me tell you. The longest English word is 'smiles.'"

Da Niu disagreed: "'Smiles' has only six letters, and how can it be longer than the fifteen-letter 'acknowledgement'?"

Er Niu said, "Assuming each letter has a length of a foot. The word 'acknowledgement' has the length of 15 feet. As for 'smiles,' from the first 's' to the second 's' the distance is one mile, or 5,280 feet."

Da Niu 恍然大悟,[340] "Thus, 'smiles' is 5,282 feet long!"

Er Niu took an English dictionary, and found "mileage" and "milestone." She said, "Actually, if 'smiles' is 5,282 feet long, 'mileage' will be 5,283, 'milestone' will be 5,285 and 'milestones' will be 5,286 feet long. The longest word 'milestones' is still not in the dictionary."

Da Niu said, "If two planets are apart very faraway, and even light from planet A needs a full year to reach planet B, the distance must be many, many times more than a mile. The word that defines this distance might be the longest word in English."

"What you mean is 'light-year,' but it is a compound word," said Er Niu. Da Niu eventually agreed with her sister, "A light-year is a huge distance, but if you count a foot a letter, it is only 10 feet long if the dash is also counted a foot. You know, both 'light' and 'year' have nothing to do with dimension."

---

[340] 恍 huǎng || huang \ all of a sudden; suddenly. 然 rán || jan \ (adverb or adjective suffix). 大 dà || ta \ greatly; fully; big; large; great. 悟 wù || wu \ realize; awaken. 恍然大悟: Suddenly realize something. (Idiom #340)

§59

Who Would Give Up Eating
for Fear of Choking

Xiao Tao did not understand what his sisters had talked about, and he was frank: "I feel English is not easy to learn either. I don't want to learn it."

Mom said, "In the world the easiest things are eating and putting on your clothes. 饭来张口, 衣来伸手.[341] How easy it will be! But someone will choke on his food, and some cowards might even 因噎废食.[342] 知难而进[343] gradually make primitive men modern men; on the contrary, always shrink back from difficulties can let modern men degenerate to primitive men."

---

[341] 饭[飯] fàn || fan \ cooked rice. 来 lái || lai \ come; arrive. 张[張] zhāng || chang \ open. 口 kǒu || k'ou \ mouth. 衣 yī || i \ clothing. 伸 shēn || shên \ stretch; extend. 手 shǒu || shou \ hand. 饭来张口, 衣来伸手: Have only to open one's mouth to be fed and hold out one's arms to be dressed—lead an easy life with everything being taken care of. (Idiom #341)

[342] 因 yīn || yin \ because of; as result of. 噎 yē || yeh \ choke. 废[廢] fèi || fei \ give up; abandon. 食 shí || shih \ eat; eating; meal; food. 因噎废食: Give up eating for fear of choking—forgo necessities in order to avoid minor risks; be extremely risk-adverse. (Idiom #342)

[343] 知 zhī || chih \ know; realize; be aware of. 难[難] nán || nan \ difficulty; hardship; trouble. 而 ér || êrh \ and yet; but; while on the other hand. 进[進] jìn || chin \ advance; move forward; move ahead. 知难而进: Advance in the face of difficulties; continue on despite knowing the hardship ahead. (Idiom #343)

When Xiao Tao expressed that he was willing to learn English, mom continued to say: "To learn something, you shouldn't 囫囵吞枣. [344]You must read the text carefully, and not glance over them without properly digesting them."

Er Niu said, "Of course, no one can swallow a date whole, otherwise it will grow into a date palm or a jujube tree in his stomach!" Everybody laughed.

---

[344] 囫 hú || hu \ whole; in one lump. 囵[圇] lún || lun \ complete. 囫囵: whole. 吞 tūn || t'un \ swallow; gulp down. 枣[棗] zǎo || tsao \ jujube; date. 囫囵吞枣: Swallow a date whole—take in information without understanding it. (Idiom #344)

§60

Time and Tide Wait for No Man

Dad said to his children, "The sea of learning has no boundary. 少壮不努力, 老大徒伤悲.[345]You should study hard!"

Mom also said, "一寸光阴一寸金, 寸金难买寸光阴.[346]You three kids should launch a competition to see who can learn nicely and quickly."

Er Niu went to take a writing brush and several pieces of paper, and wrote "时不我待"[347]four big characters. Her neat handwriting won praises.

---

[345] 少 shào || shao \ young. 壮 zhuàng || chuang \ strong; robust. 不 bù || pu \ no; not. 努 nǔ || nu \ put forth (strength); exert (effort). 力 lì || li \ power; strength; ability. 努力: make great efforts; try hard; exert oneself. 老 lǎo || lao \ old; aged. 大 dà || ta \ big (in age); large. 徒 tú || t'u \ only; vainly. 伤[傷] shāng || shang \ be distressed; hurt; injure. 悲 bēi || pei \ sad; sorrowful; melancholy. 伤悲 = 悲伤: sad; grieved; sorrowful. 少壮不努力, 老大徒伤悲: One who wastes his time during his youth will regret it when he is old—laziness in youth spells regret in old age. (Idiom #345)

[346] 一 yī || i \ one. 寸 cùn || ts'un \ a unit of length (= 33.3 mm = 1.312 inch). 光 guāng || kuang \ light; ray; brightness; luster. 阴[陰] yīn || yin \ overcast; shade. 光阴: time. 金 jīn || chin \ gold. 难[難] nán || nan \ difficult; hard; hardly possible. 买[買] mǎi || mai \ buy; purchase. 一寸光阴一寸金, 寸金难买寸光阴: An inch of time is an inch of gold, but an inch of gold can hardly buy an inch of time; money can't buy time; time is more precious than money. (Idiom #346)

[347] 时[時] shí || shih \ time; times; days; hour; opportunity; chance. 不 bù || pu \ no; not. 我 wǒ || wo \ I; we; self. 待 dài || tai \ wait for; await. 时不我待: Time does not wait for us —time and tide wait for no man. (Idiom #347)

Da Niu was 不甘落后.[348]She took the writing brush, 龙飞凤舞 [349]wrote "世上无难事, 只怕有心人."[350]

Mom said happily to Xiao Tao, "See, your sisters have made progress since you left. 士别三日, 当刮目相看.[351]What can you show us? Now is your turn!"

Xiao Tao could not write a lot. He knew he was inferior to his sisters, but he still scrawled "失败为成功之母."[352]

---

[348] 不 bù || pu \ no; not. 甘 gān || kan \ willingly; of one's own accord. 落 luò || lo \ fall. 后[後] hòu || hou \ back; behind; rear. 落后: fall behind; lag behind. 不甘落后: Not willing to lag behind. (Idiom #348)

[349] 龙[龍] lóng || lung \ dragon. 飞[飛] fēi || fei \ fly. 凤[鳳] fèng || fêng \ phoenix. 舞 wǔ || wu \ dance. 龙飞凤舞: Like dragons flying and phoenixes dancing—an ornate style of calligraphy. (Idiom #349)

[350] 世 shì || shih \ the world. 上 shàng || shang \ (used after a noun) on. 世上: in the world; on earth. 无 [無] wú || wu \ not have; there is not. 难[難] nán || nan \ difficult; hard; hardly possible. 事 shì || shih \ matter; affair; thing. 只 zhǐ || chih \ only; merely. 怕 pà || p'a \ fear; be afraid of. 有 yǒu || yu \ have; there is; exist. 心 xīn || hsin \ heart. 人 rén || jên \ person; people. 有心人: a person who sets his mind on doing something useful. 世上无难事, 只怕有心人: Nothing in the world is too difficult for one who is determined. (Idiom #350)

[351] 士 shì || shih \ scholar. 别 bié || pieh \ leave; part. 三 sān || san \ three; several. 日 rì || jih \ day. 当[當] dāng || tang \ should; must. 刮 guā || kua \ scrape. 目 mù || mu \ eye. 相 xiāng || hsiang \ each other; one another; mutually. 看 kàn || k'an \ see; look at. 刮目相看: rub eyes to see; look at somebody with new eyes; treat somebody with increased respect. 士别三日, 当刮目相看: A scholar who has been away for three days must be looked at with new eyes (must be treated with increased respect) [usually assumes that the scholar has learned new information.] (Idiom #351)

[352] 失 shī || shih \ lose. 败[敗] bài || pai \ be lose; defeat; fail. 失败: be defeated; lose; fail. 为[為] wéi || wei \ become; be. 成 chéng || ch'êng \ accomplish; succeed. 功 gōng || kung \ merit; exploit; achievement. 成功: succeed; success. 之 zhī || chih \ <auxiliary word> (used between an attribute and the word it modifies.) 母 mǔ || mu \ mother. 失败为成功之母: Failure is the mother of success—failure may prelude success. (Idiom #352)

151

§61

He Laughs Best Who Laughs Last

The two sisters laughed at Xiao Tao for his lousy writing, but he said, "What can you laugh at? A man should 能文能武.[353]I am no good in writing, but I have learned a lot during my trip. Tomorrow I will go to school to make up what I have lost, 谁笑到最后, 谁才笑得最好!"[354]

"Good, good, good! You should help each other, and 取长补短."[355]Mom and dad put their hands on the shoulders of their kids smilingly.

---

[353] 能 néng || nêng \ able; capable; can; be able to; be capable of. 文 wén || wên \ intellectual/literary skill. 武 wǔ || wu \ physical/military. 能文能武: Be masterly in both polite letters and martial arts; be good at both intellectual and physical things. (Idiom #353)

[354] 谁[誰] shuí || shui (or shéi || shei): who. 笑 xiào || hsiao \ smile; laugh. 到 dào || tao \ up until; up to. 最 zuì || tsui \ <adverb> (used in comparing several things, meaning "the most"). 后[後]hòu || hou \ later; after; afterwards. 才 cái || ts'ai \ not unless; not until. 得 de || tê \ <auxiliary word> (used to link a verb or an adjective to a complement which describes the manner or degree) 好 hǎo || hao \ good; fine; nice; well. 谁笑到最后, 谁才笑得最好: The one who can laugh through to the end must be the best laugher—He laughs best who laughs last. (Idiom #354)

[355] 取 qǔ || ch'ü \ take; get; fetch; adopt. 长[長] cháng || ch'ang \ strong point; forte; long. 补 [補] bǔ || pu \ mend; patch; repair; fill. 短 duǎn || tuan \ weak point; fault; short. 取长补短: Learn from others' strong points to make up for one's weak points. (Idiom #355)

Dad said to mom, "Our kids are all 青出于蓝而胜于蓝."[356]Mom also felt proud of her beloved children.

Dad said, "Xiao Tao needs to go a long way to make up the missed lessons, but this is OK. Listen, when I was young, my teacher taught us students a song, and the words of the song were written by a famous ancient poet and writer 陶渊明 (Tao Yuan Ming, táo yuān míng || t' ao yüan ming, 365-427). Today I can still remember it."

"Why don't you sing it?"

Dad then started to sing:

"盛年不重来, (The prime of life will not come twice,)
一日难再晨. (And one day never has two mornings.)
及时当勉励, (We urge ourselves without delay,)
岁月不待人. (Time and tide wait for no man.)"

---

[356] 青 qīng || ch'ing \ blue or green. 出 chū || ch'u \ go or come out. 于 yú || yü \ from. 出于: stem from; start from; proceed from. 蓝[蓝] lán || lan \ blue; indigo plant. 而 ér || êrh \ and yet; but; while on the other hand. 胜[勝]shèng || shêng \ (often followed by 于) surpass; be superior to. 青出于蓝而胜于蓝: Indigoblue is extracted from the indigo plant, but is bluer than the plant it comes from—the student surpasses the teacher. (Idiom #356)(Note: this idiom may be simplified as 青出于蓝)

§62

To the Satisfaction of Everyone

This was the first time for mom and the three kids to hear dad singing a song, and they felt very happy. This song was easy to learn, and therefore all of them started to sing.

"盛年不重来, (The prime of life will not come twice,)
一日难再晨. (And one day never has two mornings.)
及时当勉励, (We urge ourselves without delay,)
岁月不待人. (Time and tide wait for no man.)"

However, Er Niu who disliked singing and could not sing well actually did not sing, and she just moved her mouth as if she were singing.

"滥竽充数[357] is not allowed," said Da Niu.

"You can play the lute," mom said, "Why don't you play it?"

Er Niu then played her lute and she played very gracefully. The song sounded nice, 余音绕梁,[358] even moved animals. Someone thought that

---

[357] 滥[濫] làn || lan \ excessive; indiscriminate. 竽 yú || yü \ <music> an ancient wind instrument. 充 chōng || ch'ung \ fill; stuff; serve as ; act as ; pretend to be ; pose as. 数[數] shù || shu \ number; figure. 滥竽充数: Pass oneself off as one of the players in an ensemble—a person (or thing) who is present only to fulfill a quota (usually describes one who is incompetent or inferior). (Idiom #357)

[358] 余[餘] yú || yü \ remaining; extra; surplus. 音 yīn || yin \ sound; tone. 绕[繞] rào || jao \ wind; coil; move round. 梁[樑] liáng || liang \ roof beam; girder. 余音绕梁: The music lingering around the beams; the music leaves a lasting impression. (Idiom #358)

对牛弹琴[359]was foolish, but a cow outside was really moved by the touching song.

While singing, through the window, they saw 老牛舐犊.[360]

Xiao Tao recognized the herder was his classmate 钟华文 (Zhong Huawen, **zhōng huá wén || chung hua wên**, which means "cherish Chinese culture"), a chubby boy with bushy eyebrows and big eyes. He ran out to meet him. 久别重逢,[361]the two kids were very excited.

物以类聚，人以群分.[362]Both Xiao Tao and Zhong Huawen were naughty and cute boys, and so they became bosom friends. Xiao Tao promised to tell his whole story, and Zhong Huawen pledged to help Xiao Tao make up all his missed lessons.

Zhong Huawen said, "We should not only learn from books, but also learn through practice."

"英雄所见略同,"[363]Xiao Tao joked. It seemed that both of them considered learning by doing to be more powerful. They laughed again and again.

---

[359] 对[對] **duì || tui** \ to. 牛 **niú || niu** \ ox; cow. 弹[彈] **tán || t'an** \ play (a stringed musical instrument); plunk. 琴 **qín || ch'in** \ musical instruments (usually have strings). 对牛弹琴: Play the lute to a cow—address the wrong listener. (Idiom #359)

[360] 老 **lǎo || lao** \ old; aged. 牛 **niú || niu** \ ox; cow. 舐 **shì || shih** \ to lick; lap. 犊[犢] **dú || tu** \ calf. 老牛舐犊: An old cow fondly licking her calf—a parent being affectionate toward his or her child. (Idiom #360)

[361] 久 **jiǔ || chiu** \ for a long time. 别 **bié || pieh** \ part; leave. 重 **chóng || ch'ung** \ again; once more. 逢 **féng || fêng** \ meet; come upon. 重逢: meet again, have a reunion. 久别重逢: Meet again after a long time apart; reunite after a long separation. (idiom #361)

[362] 物 **wù || wu** \ thing; matter. 以 **yǐ || i** \ according to. 类[類] **lèi || lei** \ kind; type; class; category. 聚 **jù || chü** \ assemble; gather; get together. 人 **rén || jên** \ person; people. 群 **qún || ch'ün** \ group; crowd. 分 **fēn || fên** \ separate; divide; part. 物以类聚，人以群分: Things of same kind come together, people of same opinion fall into the same group—like attracts like; birds of a feather flock together. (Idiom #362)

[363] 英 **yīng || ying** \ outstanding person. 雄 **xióng || hsiung** \ male; grand; powerful; mighty. 英雄: hero, heroine. 所 **suǒ || so** \ <auxiliary word> (used before a verb to form a noun construction) what. 见[見] **jiàn || chien** \ see.

An old lady approached them, and introduced herself to them. "I was the first one to welcome you into this world. I am the only midwife in this area. You do not know me but I know your mothers well."

Both Xiao Tao and Zhang Huawen were embarrassed, but the midwife did not care. She searched her old-style purse and found two gifts.

"This is for you, Huawen," she gave him a small bottle of balm. "The balm smells irritating your nose, but it can drive gadflies away," said the old lady.

She then gave Xiao Tao a small comb. "This comb looks lousy, but it can keep you from head lice. Don't forget to comb your red hairs every morning!"

Xiao Tao and Zhong Huawen said "thank you" to the midwife. Her wrinkled face wreathed in smiles.

It was already late autumn, but people were in high spirits and felt spring-like. In the Guan Tian Mountain area 莺歌燕舞,[364]鸟语花香.[365]

After combing with the new comb, Xiao Tao's red hairs looked even brighter. And Xiao Tao became more handsome than before.

Looking back on his long journey, Xiao Tao truly felt that there's no place like home.

He ended his adventures with a result of 皆大欢喜.[366]

[End of Story]

略 lüè || lüeh \ somewhat. 同 tóng || t'ung \ same; alike; similar. 英雄所见略同: Great minds think alike. (Idiom #363)

[364] 莺[鶯] yīng || ying \ warbler; oriole. 歌 gē || kê \ sing; song. 燕 yàn || yen \ swallow. 舞 wǔ || wu \ dance; move about as in dance. 莺歌燕舞: Orioles sing and swallows dart—the joyfulness of spring; a happy scene of prosperity. (Idiom #364)

[365] 鸟[鳥] niǎo || niao \ bird. 语[語] yǔ || yü \ speak; say. 花 huā || hua \ flower; blossom; bloom. 香 xiāng || hsiang \ fragrant; sweet-smelling; scented. 鸟语花香: Birds sing and flowers give forth fragrance (usually as on a gorgeous spring day). (Idiom #365)

[366] 皆 jiē || chieh \ all; each and every. 大 dà || ta \ fully; greatly; big; large; great. 欢 [歡] huān || huan \ joyous; merry; jubilant. 喜 xǐ || hsi \ happy; delighted; pleased. 欢喜: joyful; happy; delighted. 皆大欢喜: All are happy; to the satisfaction of everyone. (Idiom #366)

SUMMARY OF IDIOMS
IN THIS STORY

170

174

175

185

190

REFERENCES

1.   A CHINESE-ENGLISH DICTIONARY. 1st ed. Beijing, China: Foreign Language Teaching and Research Press, 1995.

2.   WEBSTER'S NEW WORLD COLLEGE DICTIONARY. 3rd ed. Cleveland Ohio: Macmillan, Simon & Schuster, Inc., 1996.

3.   A NEW CHINESE-ENGLISH DICTIONARY. 2nd ed. Shanghai China: Shanghai *Yiwen* (Translation) Press, 1985.

4.   Yuan, Lin, and Tongheng Shen. IDIOMATIC ALLUSIONS (in Chinese), Shenyang, China: Liaoning People's Publishing House, 1982.

5.   Yang, Zhenzhong, and Renxiong Chen. THE SELECTED STORIES OF IDIOMS (in Chinese). Shanghai, China: Shanghai Educational Publishing House, 1978.

6.   Wang, Yanmei, and Xiuzhen Cheng. LEARNING IDIOMS WITH INTEREST (in Chinese). Guilin, China: Guangxi Normal University Press, 2007.